GOD'S
PARALLEL PLANETS

Jack D. Waggoner

with collaboration from *God**

---

* Who provided the author with the time, the inclination, and the imagination *and* who saw to it that this US Navy Korean veteran serving aboard the aircraft carrier USS *Philippine Sea* (CVE-47) did not have his brain and body scattered across the East China Sea, thus depriving the local fishes and bottom dwellers a succulent meal.

ISBN 978-1-64458-991-5 (paperback)
ISBN 978-1-64458-992-2 (digital)

Christian Faith Publishing, Inc.
832 Park Avenue
Meadville, PA 16335
www.christianfaithpublishing.com

Printed in the United States of America

PROLOGUE

In the beginning *God* created the heaven and the earth.

I n the Hebrew, Samaritan, and Septuagint texts, the duration from creation to the flood is calculated from a low of thirteen hundred years to a high of twenty-three hundred years; however, the Babylonians estimated it at over forty-three hundred years. Today's anthropologists maintain that humankind has been riding the blue planet around the sun for at least three hundred centuries and maybe as long as one thousand centuries. (The difference between the last two figures should prove to most that our current best estimates are only guesses.)

John McPhee, world-renowned rock breaker (geologist), Pulitzer prize winner, and friend, puts it like this in his book, *Basin and Range*, "Numbers do not seem to work well with regard to deep time. Any number above a couple of thousand years—fifty thousand, fifty million—will with nearly equal effect awe the imagination to the point of paralysis. This Triassic journey anyway is happening two hundred and ten million years ago, or five per cent back into the existence of the earth."

Genesis contains about twenty-four hundred years of history; the other thirty-eight books of the Old Testament contain about twelve hundred years which means the Old Testament totals just over thirty-six hundred years of history. Those are the facts, as we know them, but like Father Raymond Hess, priest of the Episcopal Church in Carmichael, California, says, "Most Biblical scholars say that the Hebrew scripture does not have a specific timeline. Most of the material in Genesis, chapters one through eleven, is metaphorical (symbolic, illustrative) and not meant to be literal history."

This work will assume, as some before it have, that humans arrived in their current form, between four and ten thousand years before God's twin sons were born. (Yes, twin sons! One for each of the blue planets, he placed in orbit around identical suns, in identical solar systems)

During the time from creation to the start of the Christian era, God let the parallel planets evolve from their identical starts and predictably; history on each venue followed almost identical patterns. In both worlds, the flood came and went and humans grew and expanded their scope of influence into almost every corner of each whirling blue sphere. As the Christian era came into view, humanity was a verging, semicivilized, problem-solving entity that could show great compassion for fellow beings but could also lay the neighbor's skull open with a club over the smallest dispute.

As *God*, watching his creations embrace golden idols and deities, sacrificing animals as well as fellow humans, he decided it was time to go beyond the Ten Commandments and the teachings of Abraham and all the other messengers he had introduced over the centuries. They, the human race, needed a stronger, more visual spiritual element, and the solution would be his sons. The Jesuses arrived on the parallel planets under identical circumstances, and each grew and matured, teaching and imparting God's word for the masses to assimilate.

Watching the culmination of his work, *God* was aghast, mystified, bewildered, and shocked when the leaders on each planet decided that their Jesus was a particular threat to their power and authority and unceremoniously nailed the broken bodies to crosses, insulting not only the messengers but also their creator.

God looked from planet to planet and could not fathom the diabolical, vicious, and satanic hearts that were putting his sons to death. He could let the acts play out and then raise them (his sons) from the dead and in the process give the humans on each planet redemption through the resurrection process or he could step in and prevent the cruel tortuous deaths.

On the planet earth, *God* did nothing, and two thousand years of satanical history have followed from Titus sacking Jerusalem in 70 A.D., where over a million people lost their lives to the unthinkable hijacking and crash landing of passenger jets into New York City skyscrapers (in the name of a *God*) to mark the beginning of the twenty-first century. The unconscionable action killed over three thousand people and sparked Middle East conflicts that have killed and displaced millions, bringing untold misery to a whole region of the earth's people.

On the parallel planet, *God* stepped in and sent a heavenly host of beautiful angles, divine messengers, and celestial beings to heal the wounds, revitalize the soul, and provide the planet with not only a spiritual leader but also with a mortal king that would rule the planets inhabitants in a generous and benevolent fashion from Jerusalem.

The *odd*-numbered chapters, in this work, cover an abbreviated version of earth's history and development with humankind relying only on the memory and sketchy Biblical accounts of the resurrection to spark their faith and channel their lives as Satan continues scratching at every door, every minute of every hour of every day.

The *even*-numbered chapters chronicle human history and development, on the parallel blue planet which was named *Teren*. Without Satan in the mix and with Jesus living and teaching up to current times, humankind, in the twenty-first century, has already achieved more than the earth's people could imagine, even in their wildest dreams. Jesus and God watched the people of *Teren* unlock the mysteries and wonders of their world that *God* has so skillfully hidden in the deepest recesses of each special and unique brain, and both father and son smiled in grateful, beloved satisfaction.

On Teren, millions of brains, and the bodies that nurture each, were free, over the millenniums, to expand their universe without some of the brightest and best beings destroyed in some nameless or useless war.

War—the only function of which was or is to gain control over a neighbors land and its people, thereby providing the aggressor with nothing more than pretentious and temporary regalement.

In all cases, the outcome of each particular conflict or conquest was short lived, and therefore, the loss of life, to obtain the short-lived prize, was a waste of the planets' most valuable resource: the human brain.

[*Author note*: The following is a list of the major wars from 1800 to 2000. At the end of each "earth" chapter, you will find a similar list for the time frame the chapter covers. I assume you will turn the pages quickly as it is not stimulating pros, but if you do take the time to scan the list, you will be amazed at what has taken place on the planet we ride. There is no corner of the planet except maybe the poles that has not experienced red, rich human blood slowly soaking deep into the dirt or sand and covering the rocks. Life-giving blood: turning streams and surf red and most oozing from young men whose lifeless mutilated forms stare unblinking at the sun and the stars—young men, sons of loving mothers who watched them march away with breaking hearts. Gut-wrenching goodbyes that were forever. Those that did return were never able to forget the smell of battle or the sights and sounds that were engraved so deeply into their memory tracks until they too died forever; they carry memories that would make most of us lose our lunch—memories of fallen mates, men who shared their lives and who may have save their blood from mingling with their dead comrades and their opponents. My brother-in-law, Virgil M. Watts, was a marine who saw war up close on five of the Pacific Islands during World War II. He never talked about the experience, but one day, he had been working in the yard and my sister said, "Virgil, you smell like a horse."

To which he sternly replied, "If you had used a dead enemy for a pillow, you wouldn't think I smelled bad."

The following are the recorded wars between 1800 and 2000:

Temne War (1801–1805), First Barbary War (1801–1805), War of the Oranges (1801), Stecklikrieg (1802), Tedbury's War (1802–1810), Souliote War (1803), Irish Rebellion (1803), Second Anglo–Maratha War (1803–1805), Burmese–Siamese War (1803–

1804), First Kandyan War (1803–1805), War of the Third Coalition (1803–1806), Padri War (1803–1837), Battle of Sitka (1804), First Serbian Uprising (1804–1813), Castle Hill convict rebellion (1804), Fulani War (1804–1808), Russo– Persian War (1803–1813), Egyptian Revolution (1805–1811), Janissaries' Revolt (1805), Franco–Swedish War (1805–1810), Haitian Invasion of Santo Domingo (1805), War of the Fourth Coalition (1806–1807), Russo–Turkish War (1806–1812), British invasions of the Rio de la Plata (1806–1807), Ashanti–Fante War (1806–1807), War of Christophe's Secession (1806–1811), Vellore Mutiny (1806–1811), Tican's rebellion (1807), Froberg mutiny (1807), Alexandria expedition (1807), Janissaries' Revolt (1807), Mtetwa Empire Expansion (1807–1818), Peninsular War (1807–1814), Gunboat War (1807–1814), Anglo–Russian War (1807–1812), Ottoman coups (1807–1808), Anglo–Turkish War (1807–1809), Rum Rebellion (1808–1810), Finnish War (1808–1809), Spanish Restoration in Santo Domingo (1808–18099), Dano–Swedish War (1808–1809), Travancore Rebellion (1808–1809), Gurkha–Sikh War (1809), Persian Gulf campaign (1809), War of the Fifth Coalition (1809), Gottscheer Rebellion (1809), Tyrol Rebellion (1809), Quito Revolution (1809–1810), Burmese–Siamese war (1809–1812), Bolivian War of Independence (1809–1825), Argentine War of Independence (1810–1818), Tecumseh's War (1810–1813), US occupation of West Florida (1810), Merina conquest of Madagascar (1810–1817), Punjab War (1810–1820), Chilean War of Independence (1810–1826), Conquest of Hawaii (1810), Amadu's Jihad (1810–1818), Mexican War of Independence (1810–1821), German Coast Uprising (1811), Invasion of Java (1811), Tonquin Incident (1811), Fourth Xhosa War (1811–1812), Ga–Fante War (1811), Battle of Las Piedras (1811), Cambodian Rebellion (1811–1812), Korean Revolt (1811–1812), Paraguayan Revolt (1811), Egyptian–Wahhabi War (1811–1818), Venezuelan War of Independence (1811–1823), Peruvian War of Independence (1811–1824), Battle of Shela (1812), Aponte conspiracy (1812), French invasion of Russia (1812), War of Sixth Coalition (1812–1814), War of 1812 (1812–1815), Pemmican War (1812–1821), Eight Trigrams uprising (1813), Afghan–Sikh Wars

(1813–1837), Creek War (1813–1814), Peoria War (1813), Swedish–Norwegian War (1814), Anglo–Nepalese War (1814–1816), Hadži Prodan's Revolt (1814), Argentine Civil Wars (1814–1876)(62 years), Second Barbary War (1815), Second Kandyan War (1815), Hundred Days (1815), Neapolitan War (1815), Spanish reconquest of New Granada (1815–1816), Second Serbian Uprising (1815–1817), Bussa's Rebellion (1816), Portuguese conquest of Banda Oriental (1816), Afaqi Khoja revolts (Qing dynasty) (1816–1857), Pernambucan Revolt (1817), Third Anglo–Maratha War (1817–1818), First Seminole War (1817–1818), Ndwandwe–Zulu War (1817–1819), Burmese invasions of Assam (1817–1826), Caucasian War (1817–1864), Fifth Xhosa War (1818–1819), Zulu wars of conquest (1818–1828), Sicilians' Revolution (1820), Ali Pasha's Revolt (1820–1822), Ecuadorian War of Independence (1820–1822), Trienio Liberal (1820–1823), Texas–Indian Wars (1820–1875), Wallachian uprising (1821), Niš Rebellion (1821), Ottoman–Persian War (1821–1823), Greek War of Independence (1821–1832), Padri War (1821–1837), Spanish attempts to reconquer Mexico (1821–1829), Comanche–Mexico Wars (1821–1870), War of Independence of Brazil (1822–1824), Haitian occupation of Santo Domingo (1822–1844), Demerara rebellion (1823), First Anglo–Ashanti War (1823–1831), First Greek civil war (1823–1824), Bathurst War (1824), Brazil Revolt (1824), First Bone War (1824), April Revolt (1824), Second Greek civil war (1824–1825), First Anglo–Burmese War (1824–1826), Second Bone War (1825), Aegean Sea Anti-Piracy Operations of the USA (1825–1828), Decembrist revolt (1825), Cisplatine War (1825–1828), Java War (1825–1830), Franco–Trarzan War (1825), Russo–Persian War (1826–28), Chernigov Regiment revolt (1826), Siamese–Lao War (1826–1828), Winnebago War (1827), Gran Colombia–Peru War (1828–1829), Irish and German Mercenary Soldiers' revolt (1828), Liberal Wars (1828–1834), Russo–Turkish War (1828–1829), Black War (1828–1832), Chilean Civil War (1829–1830), French Revolution (1830), Belgian Revolution (1830–1831), French conquest of Algeria (1830–1847), Port Phillip District Wars (1830–1850), Merthyr Rising (1831), Siamese–Vietnamese War (1831–1834), Baptist War (1831–1832),

Naning War (1831–1832), Egyptian–Ottoman War (1831–1833), Yagan Resistance (1831–1833), Bosnian Uprising (1831–1833), Black Hawk War (1832), French June Rebellion (1832), Albanian Revolts (1833–1839), First Carlist War (1833–1840), Peasants' Revolt (Palestine) (1834), Battle of Pinjarra (1834), Sixth Xhosa War (1834–1836), Zacatecas Rebellion Mexico (1835), Texas Revolution (1835–1836), Second Seminole War (1835–1842), Ragamuffin War (1835–1845), Cabanagem (1835–1840), War of the Confederation (1836–1839), Sabinada (1837–1838), Lower Canada Rebellion (1837–1838), Upper Canada Rebellion (1837–1838), Dutch–Ahanta War (1837–1839), Battle of Blood River (1838), Mormon War (1838), Balaiada (1838–1839), Pastry War (1838–1839), Newport Rising (1939), Egyptian–Ottoman War (1839–1841), Khivan campaign (1839), War of the Supremes (1839–1841), First Anglo–Afghan War (1839–1842), First Opium War (1839–1842), Albanian Revolt (1839–1847), Uruguayan Civil War (1839–1851), Niš Rebellion (1841), Guria rebellion (1841), Siamese–Vietnamese War (1841–1845), Sino–Sikh War (1841–1842), Shoorcha rebellion (1842), Russian Conquest of Bukhara (1842–1868), Mier Expedition (1842–1843), Albanian Revolt (1843–1844), Wairau Affray (1843), Battle of One Tree Hill (1843), Dominican War of Independence (1843–1849), Franco–Moroccan War (1844), Franco–Tahitian War (1844–1847), Albanian Revolt (1845), First Anglo–Sikh War (1845–1846), Flagstaff War (1845–1846), Hutt Valley Campaign (1845–-1846), Krakow uprising (1846), Galician Slaughter (1846), Dutch Intervention in Northern Bali (1846), Patuleia (1846–1847), Seventh Xhosa War (1846–1847), Second Carlist War (1846–1849), Mexican–American War (1846–1848), Wanganui Campaign (1846–1948), Sonderbund War (1847), Sierra Gorda Rebellion (1847–1850), Cayuse War (1847–1855), Caste War of Yucatan (1847–1933) (86 years), Italian States Revolution (1848), Greater Poland Uprising (1848), French Revolution (1848), Revolutions of German States (1848–1849), Baden Revolution (1848–1849), May Uprising in Dresden (1849), Palatine uprising (1849), Habsburg Revolutions (1848–1849), Wallachian Revolution (1848), Sicilian Revolution of Independence (1848), Dutch Intervention in Northern Bali (1848),

Matale Rebellion (1848), First Italian War of Independence (1848–1849), Second Anglo–Sikh War (1848–1849), Hungarian War of Independence (1848–1849), Serb Uprising (1848–1849), Praieira Revolt (1848–1849), Slovak Uprising (1848–1849), First Schleswig War (1848–1851), Dutch Intervention in Bali (1849–1850), Burmese–Siamese War (1849–1855), Apache Wars (1849–1924) (seventy years), Chilean Revolution (1851), Taiping Rebellion (1850–1864), Eighth Xhosa War (1850–1853), Platine War (1851–1852), Palembang Highlands Expeditions (Dutch Empire) (1851–1855), California Indian Wars (1851–1865), Nian Rebellion (1851–1868), Second Anglo–Burmese War (1852), Montenegrin–Ottoman War (1852–1853), Herzegovina Uprising (1852–1862), Crimean War (1853–1856), Epirus Revolt (1854), Revolution of Ayutla (1854–1857), Expedition against the Chinese in Montrado (1854–1855), Miao Rebellion (1854–1873), French Conquest of Senegal (1854–1860), Red Turban Rebellion (1854–1856), Bleeding Kansas Slave War (1854–1861), First Fiji Expedition (1855), Nepalese–Tibetan War (1855–1856), Santhal Rebellion (1855–1856), Yakima War (1855–1858), Rogue River War (1855), Battle of Ash Hollow (USA vs Sioux) (1855), Puget Sound War (1855–1856), Third Seminole War (1855–1858), Nias Expedition (1855–1864), Puti–Hakka Clan Wars (1855–1867), Nicaraga–Sonora War (1856), Second Opium War (1856–1860), Anglo–Persian War (1856–1857), Panthay Rebellion (1856–1873), Cheyenne Expedition (1856–1857), Indian Rebellion against British (1857–1858), Utah War (1857–1858), Ecuadorian–Peruvian Territorial Dispute (1857–1860), Reform War (1857–1861), Pahang Civil War (1857–1863), Mahtra War (1858), Coeur d'Alene War (1858), Fraser Canyon War (1858), Cochinchina Campaign (1852–1862), Indigo Revolt (1859), Second Fiji Expedition (1859), Second Italian War of Independence (1859), Chile Revolution (1859), Pig War (USA vs United Kingdom) (1859–1872), Hispano–Moroccan War (1859–1860), Banjarmasin War (Dutch vs Banjar) (1859–1863), Federal War of Venezuela (1859–1863), Italo–Sicilian War (1860), Italo–Roman War (1860), Paiute War (1860), First Taranaki War New Zealand (1860–1861), Colombian Civil War (1860–1862), Barasa–Ubaidat war (1860–

1890), Chile Occupation of Araucania (1861–1863), American Civil War (1861–1865) (six hundred and twenty thousand Americas died), French Intervention in Mexico (1861–1867), Dakota War (1862), Dungan Revolt (Muslim Rebellion, Qing Empire) (1862–1877), Ecuadorian–Colombian War (1863), Battle of Shimonoseki Straits (Japanese Civil War) (1863), Bombardment of Kagoshima (1863), Shimonoseki Campaign (1863–1864), Ambela Campaign (1863–1864), Invasion of Waikato (New Zealand) (1863–1864), Second Anglo–Ashanti War (1863), Dominican Restoration War (1863–1865), Russian–Polish Uprising (1863–1865), Colorado War (1863–1865), Second Taranaki War (New Zealand) (1863–1866), Japanese Civil War (1864), Second Schleswig War (1864), Tauranga Campaign (New Zealand) (1864), Uruguayan War (1864), Mito Rebellion (1864), Bhutan War (1864), Russo–Kokandian War (1864–1865), Chincha Islands War (1864–1866), Snake War (1864–1868), Pasoemah Expedition (Dutch) (1864–1868), Paraguayan War (1864–1870), Black Hawk War (1865–1872), Powder River Expedition (1865), Morant Bay Rebellion (1865), Hualapai War (1865–1870), Basuto–Boer War (1865–1868), Bukharan–Kokandian War (1865–1866), East Cape War (New Zealand) (1865–1868), Russo–Bukharan Wars (1865–1868), Hyogo Naval Expedition (1865), Haw Wars (Kingdom of Siam) (1865–1890), Second Choshu Expedition (1866), Austro–Prussian War (1866), Third Italian War (1866), Red Clouds War (1866), Baikal Insurrection (1866), Cretan Revolt (1866), French Campaign Korea (1866), Andaman Islands (1867), Comanche Campaign (1867–1875), Qatari-Bahraini War (1867), Klang War (1867–1874), Glorious Spain Revolution (1868), Grito de Lares Puerto Rican (1868), Titokowaru's War (New Zealand) (1869), Boshin War Japanese (1869), British Expedition to Abyssinia (1868), War of the Abyssinian Succession (1868–1872), Te Kooti's War (New Zealand) (1868–1872), Ten Years' War (Spain vs Cuba) (1868–1878), Haitian Revolution (1869), Krivosije Uprising (1869), Red River Rebellion (Canada) (1869), Franco–Prussian War (1870–1871), Kalkadoon War (1870–1890), French Civil War (1871), US Expedition to Korea (1871), Nukapu Expedition (1871), Third Carlist War (1872–1876),

Modoc War (1872–1873), Khivan Campaign Russia (1873), Aceh War (1873–1914), Pabna Peasant Uprisings (1873), Third Anglo–Ashanti War (1873–1874), Colfax County War (Apaches) (1873–1888), Cantonal Revolution (1873–1874), Brooks–Baxter War (1874), Japanese Invasion of Taiwan (1874), Red River War (1874–1875), Ganghwa Island incident (Japan) (1875), Las Cuevas War (1875), Perak War (1875–1876), Mason County War (1875–1876), Shinpuren Rebellion Japan (1876), Razlovtsi Insurrection (1876), Akizuki Rebellion Japan (1876), Hagi Rebellion Japan (1876), Colombian Civil War (1876–1877), Great Sioux War (1876–1877), Qing reconquest of Xinjiang (1876–1878), Montenegrin–Ottoman war (1876–1878), Nez Perce War (1877), Satsuma Rebellion Japan (1877), San Elizario Salt War (1877), Ninth Xhosa War (1877–1879), Russo–Turkish War (1877–1878), Kanak Revolt (1878), Kumanovo Uprising (1878), Epirus Revolt (1878), Greek Macedonian rebellion (1878), Kresna–Razlog Uprising (1878), Second Anglo–Afghan War (1878–1880), Conquest of the Desert (Argentina vs Araucans) (1878–1885), Nauruan Tribal war (1878–1888), Little War (Spain vs Cuba) (1879–1880), Jementah Civil War (1879), Anglo–Zulu War (1879), War of the Pacific (1879–1883), Sheepeater Indian War (1879), Victorio's War (1879–1881), Basuto Gun War (1880–1881), Brsjak Revolt (1880–1881), First Boer War (1880–1881), Mapuche Uprising Chile (1881), French occupation of Tunisia (1881), Mahdist War (1881–1899), Mandingo Wars (1882–1898), Timok Rebellion (1883), First Madagascar expedition (1883–1885), Tonkin Campaign (1883–1886), Chichibu Incident Japan (1884), Sino–French War (1884–1885), Mandor Rebellion (1884–1885), North–West Rebellion Canada (1885), Serbo–Bulgarian War (1885), Third Anglo–Burmese War (1885), Jambi Uprising (Dutch vs Sumatrans) (1885), Samoan Civil War (1886–1894), Karonga War (1887–1889), Hawaiian rebellions (1887–1895), Sikkim Expedition (1888), Abushiri Revolt (1889), Edi Expedition Dutch (1890), First Franco–Dahomean War (1890), Hunza–Nagar Campaign (1891), Anglo–Manipur war (1891), Chilean Civil War (1891), Garza Revolution (1891–1893), Semantan War (1891–1894), Second Hazara Uprising (1892), Congo Arab

War (1892–1894), Battle of Al Wajbah (1893), Franco–Siamese War (1893), Macedonian Struggle (1893–1908), First Melillan Campaign Spain (1893–1894), Revolta da Armada Brazilian (1893–1894), Nitrate War (1879–1884), Sino–Japanese War (1894–1895), Spanish–American War (1898), Boxer Rebellion (1899–1900), Second Boer War (1899–1902), Russo–Japanese War (1904–1905), Italo–Turkish War (1911–1912), First Balkan War (1912–1913), Second Balkan War (1913), First World War (1914–1918), Russian Civil War (1917–1922), Anglo–Afghan War (1919), Russo–Polish War (1920), Greece–Turkey War 1920–1922), Abyssinian War (1935–1936), Spanish Civil War (1936–1939), Sino–Japanese War (1937), Second World War (1939–1945), Greek Civil War (1945–1949), Chinese Civil War (1945–1949), Indonesian War of Independence (1945–1949), French Indochina War (1946–1954), Huk Revolt (1946–1954), Malagasy Revolt (1947–1948), Israeli War of Independence (1948–1949), Karen Revolt (1948–1950), Malayan War (1947–1948), Korean War (1950–1953) Indonesian Civil War (1950–1965), Tunisian War (1953–1956), Mau Uprising (1952–1960), Moroccan War (1953–1956), Tibetan Revolt (1954–1959), Algerian War (1954–1962), Cypriot War (1955–1959), Hungarian Revolt (1956), Suez–Sinai War (1956), Cuban Revolution (1956–1959), Vietnam War (1959–1975) The Congo (1960–1970), Eritrean Revolt (1960), Bay of Pigs Invasion (1961), Yemeni Civil War (1961–1970), Angolan War (1961–1975), Indo–Chinese War (1962), Cypriot Civil War (1963–1964), Malaysia–Indonesian War (1963–1966), Aden War (1963–1967), Guinean War (1963–1974), Mozambican War (1964), Indo–Pakistani War (1965), Rhodesian War (1965–1980), Arab–Israeli Six Day War (1967), Guatemala Civil War, (1967–1970), Invasion of Czechoslovakia (1965), Indo–Pakistani War (1971), Arab–Israeli War (1973), Turkish Invasion of Cyprus (1974), Angolan Civil War (1975–1976), Lebanese Civil War (1975), Namibian War (1976), Ethio-Somali War (1977–78), Sahel War (1978), Vietnamese Invasion of Kampuchea (1978–1979), Tanzanian Invasion of Uganda (1979), Russo–Afgan War (1979–1981), El Salvador Civil War (1980), Iran–Iraq Gulf War (1980), Falklands War (1982), Gulf War (1990–1991), Rwandan Civil War

(1990–1993), Tuareg Rebellion (1990–1995), Mindanao Crisis (1990), Ten Day War Slovenia (1991), Croatian War of Independence (1991–1995), Sierra Leone Civil War (1991–2002), Algerian Civil War (1991–2002), Somali Civil War (1991–ongoing), Georgian Civil War (1991– 1993), Uprisings in Iraq (1991), East Prigorodny Conflict (1992), Afghanistan Civil War (1992–1996), War in Abkhazia (1992–1993), Bosnian War (1992–1994), Civil War in Tajikistan (1992–1997), Burundian Civil War (1993–2005), Iraq Kurdish Civil War (1994–1997), First Chechen War (1994–1996), Cenepa War Peru (1995), Nepalese Civil War (1996–2006), Afghanistan Civil War (1996–2001), First Congo War (1996–1997), Kosovo War (1998–1999), Second Congo War (1998–2003), War in Afghanistan (2001–ongoing), First Ivorian Civil War (2002–2007), and the Taliban Insurgency part of the War in Afghanistan (2001–2014–ongoing). These are the five hundred fifteen primary conflicts since 1800.

In all these death-dealing engagements, plus the millions of smaller undocumented human-killing actions that have taken place on almost every square foot of our planet, inquisitive, thoughtful, and brilliant brains were blown and hacked to pieces, and the little pink brain globs scattered out across the blood and gut-drenched killing venues, from Afghanistan to Zaire, became nothing more than rat food, fish food, or mulch.

What might have come out of those millions upon millions of lost and destroyed brains?

We may find out as we take a tantalizing glimpse into life on:

God's Parallel Planets

[Author chooses to have the continents, oceans, mountains, rivers, geographic areas, regions, countries, states, cities, towns, villages, and their place names be the same on each of the parallel planets. It would be confusing to have earth's "Jerusalem" called by a different name on the parallel planet of Teren.]

1

Earth: 1 to 199 A.D.

Astronomers generally agree that the universe is expanding and has been since the beginning of time. Their studies of the heavens, by sophisticated telescopes and instruments that monitor radio waves, infrared light, ultraviolet light, X-rays, and gamma rays, all prove that we really know very little about our vast surroundings. One long-time astronomer, Jay M. Pasachoff, put it this way in *Peterson First Guide to Astronomy*: "Our view is like that of someone standing on a raisin in raisin bread dough that is rising. No matter which raisin you stand upon, all the other raisins are moving away from you."

The spacecrafts we have sent to what some call deep space may add to our knowledge, but in the overall scheme, when considering the scale, we actually have probed no further than an ant attempting to map and explore Ayers Rock in an afternoon.

The planet we ride through the vast black darkness has a parallel in a cosmos so far removed that our minds have no way to even comprehend the distance, but to the creator, who put it all in motion, it is a mere head turn to be compared and analyzed as each planet circles its own life-giving sun. With God's guidance, the parallel planets have managed to dodge life-altering or for that matter life-eliminating perils every day since first being set into motion within their duplicate solar systems. A wayward comet or asteroid, no bigger than Long Island, could alter our orbit, could change the planet's rotation, or could even so pollute the atmosphere that life could no longer exist on the blue planet as we know it today. That, however, would bring God's plan to a close and the thousands of years of watching and studying man's reaction to unfolding events would also come to an end, so the power that put all we know into motion will most likely not let that happen.

The brains our creator gave us have recently let us conquer the extremely difficult and complex problems associated with landing a space probe on a moving comet. With this proven capability, we have taken a small step toward helping control our planet's safety, at least from that one particular source of danger.

All one has to do is to look at the moon, and it's obvious that most of the surface is covered by what appear to be impact craters—big and little pieces of space debris that, over the millenniums, have smashed and crashed into the moon's surface. (For an up-close view of a meteor crater, you can drive to Arizona and walk around Barringer Crater (also known as meteor crater) which is a 560-foot deep hole that is three thousand and nine hundred feet in diameter. Experts estimate the meteor crashed into North America over fifty thousand years ago.) Scientists are certain that other meteors have struck planet earth, but when you look at the peppered moonscape, it's not hard to imagine what earth might look like if God had not had the moon running interference.

As spaceship earth orbits its sun, in a constant and mathematical way, the events unfolding after the death of Jesus Christ are truly a two-edged sword for the human race. The Roman authorities having successfully eliminated the "Jesus threat" can now continue toward the ultimate goal of ruling the planet from Rome, with no interference or distractions from someone claiming to be the son of God.

The details of the death and resurrection of Jesus are set forth in the Gospel passages as detailed by Mark 15:33 to 16:8, John 19:29 to 20:18, Matthew 27:52 to 28:20, and Luke 23:44 to 24:12, and by combining these accounts, a common story can be developed. These writings, however, come much later, and in the immediate period, after Jesus Christ's death, Rome marches forward not the least bit concerned. Government leaders, like Pontius Pilate, Archelaus, Ambivius I, and Gratus IV are totally convinced that the story of Jesus of Nazareth will soon be forgotten, by the few that he touched.

Most of the recorded wars, battles, and conflicts during the first century involved the Roman Empire, and in most, they were victorious.

In 5 A.D., Tiberius engaged Germania and consolidated the conquered territory into the empire; however, in 9 A.D., three Roman legions were annihilated in the Teutoburg Forest battles by the German hordes. In 14 A.D., the Rhine Legions mutinied upon learning of the death of Augustus but the Germanicus Caesar quelled the uprising, but not before tens of thousands died. Augusts' death brought his Golden Age to an end, but his tradition was followed by Caesar's: Tiberius, Calgula, Claidois, Nero, Vespasian, Titus, Otho, Vitellius, Flavius Domitian, and Nerva who closed out the first one hundred years after the crucifixion.

During these reigns, the Colosseum was started, in 75 A.D. by Vespasian and was finished by his son Titus just five years after groundbreaking. The venue was not only the showplace of the empire but also became a symbol to the masses of the wealth and importance of the empire.

Some historians mark the beginning of the Christian Era as commencing in the middle of the fourth year of the one hundred and ninety-fourth Olympiad, the seven hundred and forty-third year since the building of Rome and 4714 of the Julian period.

By 48 A.D., the population of Rome was estimated at almost seven million, and the empire controlled well over twenty-five million. In 79 A.D., Vesuvius erupted and Pomei and Herculaneum were buried with great loss of life and treasure, but Rome took little notice and continued down the road toward world domination.

During the fast decades of the first century after the crucifixion/resurrection, the religious leaders and holy men of the known world jockeyed for positions of leadership, and during this period Christianity and Judaism split. Split might not be the right word as many scholars believe that the two faiths may have developed on parallel paths rather than splintering off one main belief group.

Judaism existed before Christ came upon the scene as did many other religious offshoots, but in the end, Rabbinic Judaism and Proto–Orthodox Christianity where the two dominant and surviving forces. However, they did not really come into their own until well after the end of the first century, according to scholars like Daniel Boyarin.

Some argue that few Jews joined the Christian movement in the first century and that, in total, the numbers probably never exceed one thousand Jewish/Christian members. By the end of the first century, it has been estimated that there were fewer than seven thousand and five hundred Christians worldwide.

Writers like S.J.D. Cohen maintain that early Christianity ceased to be a part of the Jewish sect when it ceased to observe Jewish practices like circumcision and did not follow the tax laws, in that anyone Rome perceived to be Jewish was taxed.

In the final analysis, what set Christians apart from Jews was their faith in Christ as the resurrected messiah and the son of God. Of course, the belief in a resurrected Messiah is unacceptable to Jews of the past or present, and this one fact certainly explains part of the divisions between Judaism and Christianity.

Nowhere can one find a definitive answer as to exactly when Christianity emerged as a new religion. Some say Jesus and his message attracted both Jewish and Gentile converts but turning from attraction to a bona fide religious order is a huge step. In the period between 130 and the end of the decade, some Christians were still part of the Jewish community right up until the time of the Bar Kochba revolt.

The revolt, where it is estimated that two hundred thousand to four hundred thousand Jewish militiamen were killed, was led by three Roman legions (Legio XXII Deiotariana, Legio IX Hispana, and Legio X Fretensis). The Roman armies sustained heavy casualties but in the end were victorious in putting down the revolt that erupted as a result of religious and political tensions in Judea that followed the failure of the Jews First Revolt which had taken place in 66 A.D.

The revolt (*war*) resulted in the extensive depopulation of Judean communities, and according to some sources, five hundred and eighty thousand Jews perished from battlefield actions, and thousands more died of hunger and disease. In addition, many Judean war captives were sold into slavery, and this had a long lasting and devastating effect on all Jewish communities.

The Roman legions were seriously depleted by the war as well, and the Emperor Hadrian was so upset that he wiped the name of Judea or Ancient Israel off the map and replaced it with Syria Palestine.

The Bar Kokhba revolt greatly influenced the course of Jewish history and the philosophy up to present day. Hadrian's death in 138 seemed to signal a pause in Jewish persecution; however, the Romans barred Jews from Jerusalem, and even Jewish Christians were banned from the city.

Historians cite many reasons for the revolt; however, most agree that the primary elements were the diffuse presence of Romans, alterations in agricultural practice where a shift from land ownership to sharecropping took place, a period of sever economic decline, and an upsurge of nationalism. Another key factor was Hadrian's plans to build a new city called Adelia Capitolina over the ruins of Jerusalem and the erection of a temple to Jupiter on the temple mount site.

When all the Roman actions were tallied, the details showed the destruction of fifty fortified Jewish towns, nine hundred and eighty-five villages razed to the ground, and over six hundred thousand Jews killed or displaced.

Over the centuries, the Bar Kokhba Revolt became a symbol of Jewish pride, and David Ben-Gurion, Israel's first prime minister, took his Hebrew last name from one of Bar Kokhba's leading generals.

As the second century got underway, the world found Rome in Britannia building the Roman Wall. It was a defensive fortification that started in 122 A.D. under the reign of Emperor Hadrian. The wall was almost eighty miles long and was completed in just six years. Roman legions and conscripted locals were used to construct the mostly rock and dirt escarpment.

In the years after Hadrian's death, in 138 A.D., the new emperor, Antonnius Pius, essentially abandoned the wall and started building the Antonnine Wall about one hundred and sixty kilometers north, in the area which later became known as the Scottish Lowlands. Neither wall was ever of much tactical use, and during the reign of Marcus Aurelius, the opposing forces went back and forth vying for control over the surrounding lands. By the time Septimius Severus (108-211) tried to conquer Caledonia, the walls were of no value, and by the fourth century, the Roman rule in Britain ended, and the local governments where left to look after their own defenses.

By the end of the second century, after the death of Christ, earth was continuing along the line it had been following for thousands of years. The dominant regional group would mount a war to acquire territory and to expand their influence and to enslave their enemies.

For example, in Asia, the Chinese dynasties of Nang Mang, Quang Vouti, Ming-ti, and Thang-ti all consolidated their powers and started negotiations with the Pathian Empire to initiate trade between the two far-flung peoples; thus the Silk Road is established. It flourishes under changing leadership, on both sides, right up until 1265, when Maffeo Polo arrived off the China coast and initiated the water trade routes that continue today.

Around 80 A.D., the Kushan dynasty was established, and it operated out of two capitals: Purshapura (now Peshawar) near the Khyber Pass and the city of Matur in Northern India. The Kanishka's rulers controlled a large territory ranging from the Aral Sea through the areas that include present-day Uzbekistan, Afghanistan, Pakistan, and northern India as far east as Benares and as far south as Sanchi. It was a period of great wealth marked by extensive mercantile activities and a flourishing of urban life where Buddhist thought and visual arts were given high priorities.

Rome may have been the dominant force around the Mediterranean, but in Asia Minor, the Parthian Empire (Sixth Oriental Monarch) also known as the Persian Empire was on the move. From well before the Christian era, they controlled large portions of the world from their base in Syria. The Seleucid family acquired most of the land that Alexander the Great conquered, and from this base, they focused their attention on the constant rivalries with the kings of Egypt, Macedonia, and the other states in the

Hellenistic world. By the beginning of the third century, the Parthian empire was on the downhill slope, and various factions eagerly carved up the lands that had been controlled by the Parthian King Artabanus IV.

Not all of life was war and killing. On the educational side, Ptolemy Claudius was an influential astronomer, geographer, and mathematician of the ancient world. He was of Greek descent but lived in Alexandria, Egypt, between 85 A.D. and 165 A.D. He was the first to advance the theory that the earth was the center of the universe and that the sun and stars revolved around the planet, just like our moon. His teachings and maps were used as textbooks well into the 1400s, and his book, the *Amagest,* shares with Euclid's *Elements,* the glory of being the scientific text longest in use. From its conception in the second century up to the late Renaissance, Ptolemy Claudius' manual was the scientific bible of astronomy. The following is an epigram accepted by many as having been written by Ptolemy:

> Well do I know that I am mortal, a creature of one day. But if my mind follows the winding paths of the stars Then my feet no longer rest on earth, but standing by Zeus himself I take my fill of ambrosia, the divine dish.

The world population, at this point, is estimated to be around one hundred and ninety-five million. The death and destruction carried out by the Romans and all the other worldwide power-seeking groups, trying to inch up the ladder or to cement their existing power, resulted in the death of hundreds of thousands, if not millions, of people, in the short time span of just two hundred years.

The recorded wars were Bellum Batonianum (6), Battle of the Teutoburg Forest (9), Goguryeo–Dongbuyeo Wars (6–21), Marodobuus War with Arminius (17), Lulin Rebellion (17), Tacfarinas Rebellion (24), Red Eyebrows Rebellion (26), Trung sisters' rebellion (42), Roman conquest of Britain (43-46), War between Armenia an Iberia (50), Hermunduri–Chatti War (58),

Roman–Parthian War (58-63), Boudica's Uprising (60), First Jewish-Roman War (66–73), Year of the Four Emperors (69), Revolt of the Batavi (69), Battle of Yiwulu (69), Destruction of the Xiongnu state (89–93), First Dacian War (101), Second Dacian War (105), Kitos War (115), Bar Kokhba Revolt (132–136), Roman–Parthian War (161-166), Marcomannic Wars (166–180), Yellow Turban Rebellion (184–205), Campaign against Dong Zhuo (190), Year of the Five Emperors (193), Sun Ce's conquest in Jiangdong (194- 199), Clodius Albinus Failed Usurpation (197).

Wars: 31

2

Teren: 1 to 199

On *Teren,* in the first two-hundred years after the crucifixion and the saving of Jesus, by the angels, archangels, divine messengers, heavenly beings, and the supernatural spirits, there was a change so dramatic, relative to human action, reaction, and interaction that not even Nostradamus could have foreseen the cataclysmic demise of what had been the normal institutions, i.e., those previously devised by man, in his efforts to gain control over his neighbors and their wealth and territories. The divine presence that Jesus's hands-on CEO leadership had on mankind was truly mind altering. As humans normally resist change and long for the old proven ways, they were shown, in short order, that God's plan for the future was well designed and would give everyone a better, more productive, and happier life. It was not that there would no longer be weak and vulnerable people, but that the strong spiritual leaders, appointed by Jesus, would treat all their charges with dignity and respect which is really all that most human beings want or require.

As the first and then the second centuries flashed by, Jesus took his message and God's Ten Commandants around the world and preached his message to the locals in the mountains of Peru, the islands of the Pacific, to the vast river valleys of Asia, and everywhere in-between. He appeared in each remote corner of the world, courtesy of his angel transport, and when he left an area, the population spoke his tongue and would from that point forward. They were also

Christian, i.e., they saw the error of their idol and deity worship, and the miracles he performed, proved beyond doubt, that he could be no one but the son of the creator God.

With all the peoples of the world speaking and writing the same language and following the same set of commandments, the inter-tribal action, as the result of exploratory chance meetings, blended the human race into one homogenous family, and different local customs and traditions did not seem so foreign or threatening.

Cities, towns, hamlets, and family groupings devised local governments based on a format established by Jesus and his leadership council. The spiritual and community leaders, who were in all cases men of God, but then all the people on the planet fit that category, used common sense and were guided by the golden rule and the Ten Commandments. The bible did not exist; however, Jesus did make use of parables to explain and expand on the laws that God had given Moses, and his teachings and pronouncements were contained in a volume called "God's Laws*". The subordinates, appointed by Jesus, did not have the power of life or death nor was there any need for such harsh and draconian measures. Communities came together to provide the infrastructure that the people wanted and required, and it certainly was not what we think of when we consider socialism. When all the people in a community or region or continent were working for the betterment of society, with a common set of rules, there was almost nothing that could not be accomplished.

Funds were not spent on grand churches that took centuries to build but rather on open-air forms where the weather was conducive, like the outdoor amphitheater in Kusadasi, Turkey, that would serve as the local government's meeting places and entertainment venues for plays, concerts, and all manner of entertainment. Small taxes were imposed on each family unit, but community labor was always an option, and the communities around the planet followed the models that the Romans had designed for water, sewer, and utility support systems.

People were free to follow their dreams and passions, and lively trade activity began to link the cities and towns of each region, and eventually, it expanded into trade routes that covered the planet.

World trade, in just the first two-hundred years of Jesus's reign, soared to levels that would not be reached on earth until well after the dark ages.

This demand for the transport of goods sparked the imagination of inventors, craftsmen, and conveyances of all kind contributed to a transport renaissance that extended not only on the land trade routes but also on the sea lanes as well. Merchant cargo ships expanded their ranges from plying only coastal waters to challenging not only the Mediterranean but also the other great oceans. Shipwrights at the end of the first century were building vessels that rivaled those that headed out in the thirteenth century, on earth, to discover the new worlds.

Without fear of conscription, into some tyrannical monarchs army, young men were free to explore all manner of ways to make life more enjoyable for themselves, their family, and their fellow clansmen. Artisans and thinkers did not waste their time devising implements of war and building massive forts, castles, and defensive positions but rather put their talents and energies into finding a better way to do almost everything—from agriculture to fishing, from learning how to work metals into lasting tools to managing livestock and bringing arid land from uselessness to valuable by simply rechanneling water resources.

By the time the century had passed, years without persecution of any kind, the old ways of man became lost in the multitude of exciting and dramatic changes. By the year 100, everyone on the planet had been born under the rule and guidance of God's son, and the old trappings, of the Before Christ period, were nothing but interesting artifacts. The Parathion, the Coliseum, the signature buildings of the Roman Empire were just places to visit and remember how different life had been before the coming of God's beloved son.

By the year 200, the population of Teren was almost ten percent larger than the earth (around two hundred and fifteen million) in that people only died from old age or from disease and plague. There were no murders, there were no young men marching off to some nameless war, and there was no starvation; there was only the hum of human activity all done, all undertaken within the confines of a benevolent society. God looked down on his beloved son, with his earth son seated at his right side, and could not have been more pleased. The first two hundred years of the parallel planet was a huge success, and God could not wait to see what the future would bring forth from the human brains that were only controlled and guided by the Ten Commandments and the Golden Rule. Mankind proved over and over again that among God's creatures, he was the most inquisitive and capable. Collective minds came together to solve age-old problems, and why not, they were well fed and well-educated, and there were no satanic distractions.

Wars: None.

*Example of Jesus hands-on teachings. The words of the Christ were contained in the *God's Laws* book that was updated as Jesus guided his flock through the centuries. Pronouncements similar to 2 Peter 1:5–8: "Make every effort to add to your faith goodness; and to goodness, knowledge; self-control; and to self-control, perseverance; and to perseverance, godliness: and to godliness, brotherly kindness; and to brotherly kindness, love. For if you possess these qualities in increasing measure, they will keep you from being ineffective and unproductive in your knowledge of our God."

---

* Christ Assumes Authority

3

Earth: 200 to 399 A.D.

During the second, third, and into the fourth centuries, human development centered on the Roman Empire. From Augustus Caesar (30 B.C.) to Augustus Romulus (476 A.D.), all roads, did indeed, lead to Rome and it's expanding golden empire.

However, Roman retractions were taking place all over the empire, and in the rule of Commodus, the Goths (East Germanic people) played an important part in the fall of the Western Roman Empire and the emergence of Medieval Europe. The Goths sacked and burned the Temple of Diana in 260 A.D. and burned Athens in 263 A.D. They increasingly became soldiers in the Roman armies in the fourth century contributing to the almost complete Germanization of the Roman Army. In Constantinople, the Gothic leaders were heavily criticized for their penchant for wearing skins, but in time, it became the fashion in not only Constantinople but also the rest of the empire as well.

During these years of dramatic change, scholars estimate that most books of the New Testament had already been written. Some of the writings were being circulated within the learning centers of the world; however, they were not assembled or cataloged, just put into circulation as historical journals and papers of interest.

The New Testament (twenty-seven books in one volume) was written by at least eight different authors, none of whom had direct physical contact with Jesus during his time on earth. The individual books and the resulting consolidation began to gain wide attention within the civilized world by the early 200s, and in some quarters, it was described as, "Within this awful volume lies the mystery of mysteries."

Jewish–Christians, that is, Jewish disciples of Christ who lived in the Roman Empire under Roman occupation, were the primary authors. The one exception may have been Luke who some scholars think was a Hellenistic Jew or possibly a Gentile.

The Gospels' authorship has long been a subject of debate among Christian scholars, but many of the New Testament books were not written by the individuals whose names are attached. It is the perspective of many experts that none of the books were written in Palestine and that most were written in the Koine Greek language.

As Christianity spread, the books of the New Testament were translated into other languages, most notably Latin, Sriac, and Egyptian Coptic. It is generally agreed that the historical Jesus primarily spoke Arabic or perhaps some Hebrew and Koine Greek.

It is difficult if not impossible to know exactly what the authors wanted to convey from their second-, third-, or fourth-hand knowledge, but just one small translation of the anomaly gives the reader an idea of the difficulty surrounding the exact interpretations. Jewish translations often reflect traditional Jewish interpretations as opposed to the Christian understanding. For example, Jewish translators translate "aimah" in Isaiah 7:14 as "young woman," while many Christian translations render the word as virgin.

Isaiah 7:14: "Therefore the Lord himself will give you a sign: The virgin will conceive and give birth to a son and will call him Emmanuel."

The words of the bible were written, edited, translated, and printed by man. The interpretations and faith that we choose to glean from those written words, which very well may have been directed, assembled, and created by divine intervention, is a personal choice made by each reader.

Other works of the period came from scholars like Porphyry who wrote fifteen books against Christianity; Origen who, it was reported, authored over 6000 books; and Plotinus, a teacher of Platonic Philosophy who wrote twenty-six books.

Elsewhere in the world, the Persian emperor Sapor, the new emperor, inherited his father's vendetta against Rome and pursued it with vigor. At the time, Armenia was a Roman ally who Sapor overran and sacked. Valerian, the Roman emperor, assembled a force and marched through Asia Minor to lay waste to Persia itself. Sapor took advantage of a personal negotiation with the emperor by taking him prisoner. It was an outrage of diplomatic practices, but nothing could be done, and leaderless, the Roman army surrendered.

The Romans could no longer defend their borders, and Sapor took advantage by ransacking Antioch and causing as much havoc as possible in the surrounding areas, including Alexandria. He then retreated with as much wealth as he could carry, realizing that when Rome regrouped, he would be soundly trounced.

The world population was now estimated at two hundred and five million with the average citizen of Rome living to an average age of twenty to twenty-five years. If you factor out the high death rate (almost fifty percent) for children one to five, and then, the average goes up to near fifty years of life. So if you made it to your sixth or seventh year, your odds of living to fifty years old were quite good.

In Asia, the Hieu-Ti VI and VII controlled vast areas in and around the coast, but the interior was a wild and unmanageable patchwork of vicious tribes and clans that randomly rained terror on the boarding Chinese and indigenous peoples. During this period, the Quin dynasty finished the Great Wall of China to help curb these incursions by the nomads from inner Asia.

Wars recorded were Conquest of Garama (202), Roman invasion of Caledonia (208), Parthian War (216), Zhuge Liang's Northern Expeditions (228–234), Han dynasty falls, China disintegrates (220), Zhuge Liang's Campaign (228), Goguryeo Wei Wo, r (244), Jiang Weis Expeditions (247), Invasion of Raetia by Juthungi (259), Conquest of Shu Byu Wei (263), Battle of Naissus (268), Establishment of Paimyrene Empire 270), War of Emperor Aurelian (270), Conquest of Palmyrene Empire (272), Library of Alexandria destroyed by Aurelian (273), Conquest of Jack D. Waggoner Earth

(200–399 A.D.), Galic Empire (274), Conquest of Wu by Jin (279), Carausian Revolt (286), War of Eight Princes (291), Civil wars of Tetrarchy (306), War of Licinius (313), War of Constantine (314), Jewish revolt (351), Great Conspiracy (367), Gothic War (376), Tanukh revolt against Rome (378), Conquest of Alaric I (395), Visigothic Invasion of Greece (395), Stillcho's Pictish War (398), and Gildonic revolt (398).

Wars: 30

4

Teren: 200 to 399 C.A.A.

By the year 399 C.A.A. (after Christ Assumes Authority), Christ's leadership, at the spiritual and mortal levels, was rapidly turning Teren into an exciting fulfillment of God's highest expectations. Man was pioneering and exploring so many areas. There seemed to be no end or limits to his inquisitive nature where idea built upon idea with the next level always close at hand.

Ferrous metals were being mined and smelted, and all manner of tools, utensils, and implements were being fashioned from this indestructible material. Iron plows, scythe, nails, and even nuts and bolts were being used in all types of construction projects from ships to farm implements. The copper, brass, and tin alloys of the Roman years could not compare with the strength and durability of iron.

Oil was being gathered from seeps all over the world, and near Kirkuk, in present day Iraq, the black ooze was actually bubbling up out of the ground. It greased the skids of almost every trade, and new uses were discovered almost daily. By distilling the semi-liquid goo, in metal containers, kerosene was produced, and it proved to be an economical replacement for wood with regard to cooking and heating. It also provided a clean source of light, thereby extending activities into the dark hours of each daily cycle. Coal was also being mined and exported into metal manufacturing facilities and small quantities of steel were being produced using the hot fires that coke brought to the table.

In the learning centers and universities that were springing up in every region, mathematics was being explored at all levels. Geometry, trigonometry, calculus, and everything in-between were being studied, and advancements came so fast that as soon as one theory was discovered and proven to be an axiom, another level was added and the quest for understanding started, reaching beyond the planet and into the nighttime skies.

While earth was stuck in an eight-hundred-year track of thinking it was the center of the universe, the Terenlings were already advancing the theory that their planet was one of many moving in established paths around the sun and that the stars were other, distant suns. It was an easy step to imagine that those millions, maybe billions, of other suns had similar solar systems circling each white-hot dot.

The study of the heavens was given a major boost when a glass-maker noticed that a drop of water magnified whatever it rested upon and he wondered if a drop of clear glass would do the same. As mankind began to understand the magnifying power of a curved-glass surface, cultured-concave, and convex-polished glass pieces began producing more and more magnification. By linking up lenses in a tube, the microscope was born, and when it was turned toward the heavens, details beyond imagination came crashing down out of the sky, directly through the telescope and into the observer's brain. Craters on the moon, individual rocks casted shadows; it was incredible, and soon planets and stars, millions of miles away, were being catalogued and studied. It was always one of man's bedrock, ingrained human traits, that bigger is better, and when applied to the telescope, there was no turning back. By the end of the century, telescopes were being developed that were six to eight inches in diameter, and it would only be a matter of time before even larger units would bring the heavens even closer.

During these exciting times and amid thousands of innovations and advancements in every field of human endeavor, health issues were given a great deal of emphasis and startling discoveries were being made. The microscope opened up a whole new world to the health scientist, and it was soon discovered that hygiene played a big part in the overall health of each individual. Wounds cleaned with fresh clear water and treated with herbs healed faster and better than those not so cleansed. Diet was also determined to be critical to good health, and the consumption of fruits, berries, and nuts, as a part of each daily diet, lead to better overall health and resistance to the aliments and diseases that plagued many of the metropolitan centers. The country dwellers seem to be almost immune to the various plagues and diseases that ran rampant through the population centers. Only when affected city dwellers came in contact with the country folks did the disease pass, and this lead to understanding isolation and people with afflictions were thus restricted from travel, and the transmission and infestation levels were greatly reduced.

In the Asian areas, the long-time use of herbal remedies and holistic healing had advanced well beyond what the rest of the world practiced, and as the trade routes and communication systems improved, valuable remedies and cures were adopted by the medical scientist outside Asia.

The technical advancements being put forward in every industry and profession were processed through information agencies in every world population center and then funneled to a clearing house in Jerusalem. A mail system was devised to disseminate the gathered data, by the written word, to every jurisdiction on the planet, and thus, an idea hatched in Norway today could well be in the hands of similar minded people, halfway around the world, in a mere matter of months. This information system magnified and chronicled each technical and social advancement and contributed to a sharing of ideas that was unparalleled in human history.

The population of Teren ballooned to almost three hundred and fourteen million by the beginning of the fourth century under the new health and sanitation policies that were advancing so rapidly in every corner of the planet.

Wars: None.

5

Earth: 400 to 599 A.D.

I n 409, the Belgium revolt against Roman rule was just another crack in the empire that would never be repaired. At the same time, the German peoples were coming together and putting in motion their plans for independence.

In the beginning of the century (451), the Battle of Chalons or the Battle of the Catalaunian Plains was between Romans and the Huns, commanded by their king Attila. John Julius Norwich, noted historian, said of the battle of Chalons: "It should never be forgotten that in the summer of 451 and again in 452 the whole fate of western civilization hung in the balance. Had the Hunnish army not been halted, in these two successive campaigns, had its leader toppled Valentinian from his throne and set up his own capital at Ravenna or Rome, there is little doubt that both Gaul and Italy would have been reduced to spiritual and cultural deserts."

Many writers and historians agree that the battle was where a predominantly Christian force faced a predominantly pagan opponent, and many credited prayer as playing a major factor in the outcome. All told estimates of battlefield deaths range from a low of three hundred thousand to a high of half a million. The philosopher Damascius stated that the fighting was so severe "that no one survived except the leaders on either side and a few followers; but the ghosts of those who fell continued the struggle for three whole days and nights as violently as if they had been alive: the clash of their arms was clearly audible."

The year 476 signaled the formal end of the Western Roman Empire. That year, the German chief Flavius Odoacer lead a group of Germanic mercenaries and overthrew Orestes who had previously stolen power form emperor Julius Nepos. Odoacer and his men captured and executed Orestes and later captured Ravenna and killed Orestes' son Romulus Augustus. These events brought to an end the Roman Empire in the West and Odoacer quickly conquered the remaining provinces in Italy.

With Odoacer installed as the first barbarian King of Italy, a new era was initiated. Unlike most previous emperors, he acted with decisive actions, and as a result, he took tight military control over all of Italy and its neighboring areas. He even bullied the Vandal King Gaiseric to cede him Sicily, and during his reign, he had full support and cooperation from the Roman Senate.

Although Odoacer was an Arian Christian, his relations with the Chalcedonian church hierarchy were good, and to cement relationships, he arranged for the inhabitants of Liguria a five-year immunity from taxes which further enhanced his acceptance.

In 489, Odoacer met an army from Emperor Zeno at Isonzo (the same Isonzo where twelve battles took place in WW I between Austro–Hungarian and Italian armies—present-day Slovenia) and was defeated. He withdrew to Verona and set up a fortified camp, but three days later, he was again defeated and fled to Ravenna. Again, his attackers besieged Odoacer, and while he was fully engaged, the Burgundians (East Germanic or Vandal tribe from present-day Poland) seized the opportunity to plunder and devastate Liguria (a crescent-shaped region of northwest Italy on the Mediterranean coastline known as the Italian Riviera) taking many prominent citizens as hostage.

In March 493, Odoacer was killed by Theodoric who had lead all the battles against the Italian Emperor, and on the same day, Odoacer's wife, family, and any of his soldiers who could be found were also killed.

Odoacer was the first ruler of Italy for whom the original text of any of his legal acts has survived. There is a grant, by the slain king, (written on Papyrus) for properties in Sicily and on the island of Melita. Parts of the original document are now in the Biblioteca Nazionale library in Naples.

Meanwhile, in Ireland, Saint Patrick (a Christian missionary and first bishop of Ireland) was busy bringing Christianity to Ireland by converting a society that was practicing a form of Celtic polytheism. He was born in Britannia around 385 A.D. and died in Saul about 461.

One account of his early life says he was captured by Irish pirates who brought him to Ireland where he was enslaved and held captive for six years. He explained in *The Confession* that his time in captivity was critical to his spiritual development, further saying that the Lord had mercy on his youth and ignorance and afforded him an opportunity to not only escape but also to be forgiven for his sins and showed the path toward his conversion to Christianity. In one of his writings, he notes that he baptized thousands of people, ordained priests, talked wealthy women into becoming nuns, and held council with Kings. About the Irish people, he said: "Never before did they know of God except to serve idols and unclean things. But now, they have become the people of the Lord."

During the early periods, after Jesus died, church councils were traditional and the ecumenical councils were a continuation of those held earlier in the empire before Christianity was made legal. These include the Council of Jerusalem (50 A.D.), the Council of Rome (155), and councils every few years, thereafter ending with the Council of Aries in 314. The first seven ecumenical councils were an attempt to reach an orthodox consensus and to unify Christendom. Maybe the most important in this time frame was the Council of Chalcedon (451) that adopted and described the hypostatic union of the two natures of Christ, i.e., human and divine. Over the centuries, the various arms of the Protestant, Catholic, and Orthodox churches battled over the Pope's authority, or lack thereof, and each group interpreted the Christian messages, along the lines that were most comfortable for their particular beliefs and traditions.

With the Roman exit from Britain (426), all manner of tribes and groups dominated the English countryside. The well know-names of Kent, Sussex, Wessex, Essex, North Umbria, Angles, Saxon,

Wales, and Ireland all jockeyed for control and war-dominated life on the island.

The year 486 found the French Feudal system on the rise, and Spain was coming into prominence under the Visigothic Kingdom that occupied what is now southwestern France, Spain, Portugal, Andorra, Gibraltar, and Monaco. The kingdom maintained independence from the Eastern Roman or Byzantine Empire and was at times called the Kingdom of Toulouse. The Visigoths and their early kings were Arians and came into conflict with the Catholic Church but later converted, and the church exerted an enormous influence on secular affairs through the Councils of Toledo. The Visigoths also developed the highly influential law code known in Western Europe as the Liber ludiciorum, which would become the basis for Spanish law throughout the Middle Ages.

The Visigoths evolved and by 586 King Liuvigild's son Reccared I converted to Chalcedonian Christianity and announced his faith in the Nicene creed. He styled himself as the successor to the Roman emperors, but his reign was short-lived. The instability of this period can be attributed to the power struggle between the kings and the nobles. Religious unification strengthened the political power of the church, which exercised with an iron hand.

In the Byzantine Empire, the continuation of the Roman Empire in the Greek-speaking Eastern part of the Mediterranean, it was perennial war with the Muslims. It flourished during the reign of the Macedonian emperors, and its demise was the consequence of attacks by Seljuk Turks, Crusaders, and Ottoman Turks.

As Christianity in the empire became organized, the church was led by five patriarchs who resided in Alexandria, Jerusalem, Antioch, Constantinople, and Rome. The Council of Chalcedon (451) decided that the patriarch of Constantinople was to be the second in the ecclesiastical hierarchy. Only the Pope in Rome was superior.

The culture of the Byzantium population was rich and affluent, and science and technology was promoted and flourished. An important hand-me-down from the period was the Byzantine tradition of rhetoric and public debate. Philosophical and theological discourses were an important part of public life, with the emperor even taking part in the discussions. The Byzantines were also responsible for passing on Greek legacy, and this knowledge helped Europe as it entered into the beginning of the European Renaissance.

Interesting at this point in human development is that the comprehension of their surroundings was so off base. Comas, an Egyptian Monk, wrote a work called *Topography of the World*, which argued that the earth was a vast plain surrounded by an immense wall at whose side was a great mountain which concealed the sun every night.

China, long divided into north and south, is further subdivided into the northwestern and northeastern regions ruled by different factions of the once powerful Northern Wei empire. Art and literature flourished, reflecting influences from the different cultures with which China maintained trade relations. The Sui dynasty (581–618) and the Chen dynasty (557–589) remain the most powerful groups.

By this time, world population is estimated at two hundred and thirteen million and wars, since the year 400, have claimed the lives of at least six million. Wars like Visigothic First Invasion of Italy (401), Battle of Mainz(406), Visigothic Second Invasion of Italy·(408), Sack of Rome (410), Roman–Sasanian War (421), Picts invade Britain (428), Gaiseric invades Numidia (430), Chinese attacks Champa (Vietnam)(431), Battle of Ravenna (432), Hunnic invasion of Europe (434), Huns Capture Ratiaria (441), Suevian King Rechiar devastated Tarraconensis (449), Battle of Avarayr (451), Ambrosius makes war on Vortigern in Britian (437), Germanic–Hunnic Wars (453), Second Sack of Rome (455), Ricimer's army defeat Vandals (456), Battle of Cap Bon (468), Basiliscus scattered the Vandal fleet (468), Prince Hoshikawa Rebellion (479), Battle of Herat (484), Sukhra's Hephthalite campaign(484), Saxons defeated Britons at Mearedsburn (485), Conquest of Italy by Theoderic the Great (488), Rebellion of 100,000 in Isauria was defeated in Phrygia (493), Basus War (494 to 534), Saracen invasion of Syria (498), Arthur's victory over Saxons (500), Anasstasian War (502), Kavadh invaded Armenia (502), Persian–Roman Wars (503–557), Battle of Vitalian (511), Revolt of Vitalian (511), Burgundian army defeated (523), North China Civil war (523-24), Abyssinian army conquers Yemen

(525), Iberian War (526), Iwai Rebellion (527), Franks took over Thuringian (528), 25,000 Roman troops engaged 40,000 Persians (530), Battle of Unstrut (531), Niko Revolt (532), 30,000 killed in Constantinople revolt (532), Vandalic War (533), War against the Moors (534), Gothic War (535), First Tikai–Calakmui War (537), Witigis besieged the army of Belisaris at Rome (537–538), Theudebert army of Franks invaded Italy (539), Lazic War (541), Persians demolished Callinicum (542), Areobindus and Sergius defeated at Carthage (545), Marauding Sclavenes ravaged Illyricum and Thrace (549), Paekche and Silla attacked Koguryo (Korea) (551), Gothic navy defeated by fleet of John (551), Conquest of Spania (551), Battle at Taginae (552), Narses invaded Italy with army of 25,000 (552), First Tikal–Caracol War (556), Battle of Bukhara (557), Second Tikal–Caracol War (562), Silla drove Japanese of Korea mainland (562), Siege of Sana'a (570), Byzantine–Sasanian War (572), Sasanid reconquest of Yemen (575), Battle at Deorham (577), Her–Menegild's revolt (580), Sui dynasty Reunites China (581), Maurice's Balkan campaigns (582), First Perso–Turkic War (588), Goguryeo–Sui War (598), and the Frisian–Frankish wars (598–793).

Recorded wars: Seventy-two

6 *

Teren: 400 to 599

I n just six hundred years, the population of Teren was almost sixty percent more than earth, and their scientific and industrial advancements put them well past what was going on earth at the turn of the millennium or beyond. Without battlefield or violent deaths, of any kind, there are one hundred and thirty million more brains innovating, researching. experimenting, and exploring, and the advancements are so rapid and numerous that they almost trip over each other.

By 500, the sextant was a major scientific breakthrough that came from those minds that had developed the telescope. (On earth, the sextant was not developed until 1730). This instrument provided an easy and consistent way to find the latitude of one's location and contributed to the mapping and exploring of all the land masses on the planet which led to improved trade routes on both land and sea.

Telescopes were allowing the Terenlings to identify the other planets, in their solar system, and to map the stars beyond. Most universities had planetariums, and the astronomers running those facilities were some of the most respected and revered brains.

As Jesus traveled around the world, he had the pleasure of asking penetrating and leading questions—questions that were like minia-ture keys to giant locks. Simple, clever, calculating questions that

---

could set about dramatic thought sequences that could lead to new and radical, outside-the-box, thinking. Standing on the sea shore, looking out at the incredible two and three mast sailing ships plying the brilliant blue Mediterranean waters he may have asked, "I wonder if mankind will ever be able to sail over the moon like these ships sail over the horizon?" Not just a simple observation but a seed that when planted deep, within the brain, can grow and flourish, taking the listener almost anywhere.

Around 200 B.C. the Chinese, of the Han dynasty, had developed a crude compass, and by the sixth century, it had been refined and was being exported to all the developing nations of the world. It along with the sextant were making traveling the oceans and the great land masses a safe and calculated undertaking rather than the dead reckoning of the past that had left so many explorers' bones bleaching on isolated beaches, mountain, passes or desert wastelands.

With Teren's population exploding, the need for improved agriculture methods was critical, and one of the early inventions that implemented a boom in agriculture production was the horse collar. Up to this point, oxen provided the agriculture power, and while the yoke was one solution, it had its drawbacks in that the animals were not particularly powerful, and the yoke tended to choke the beast. The horse collar was a padded unit that pressed against the animal's shoulders and thus did not choke him. Use of the horse collar sped the development of transportation and greatly increased the use of the horse as a draft animal. When a horse was harnessed with the collar, the horse could apply fifty percent more power to the task than could the ox, due to the horse's greater size and speed. The use of horses in agriculture and in transportation boosted economies and reduced reliance on subsistence farming. This, in turn, allowed people more time to develop specialized activities and consequently led to the development of early industry, education, and the arts in market-based towns and cities.

By 600, transportation, the ability to move goods and people around the planet, became a driving force in the development and advancement of society on Teren. This healthy interaction between the peoples of the world was facilitated by transportation improvements, from the sleek three mast sailing ships that plied the open oceans to the multiwheeled vehicles that bumped and churned over the potholed and sometimes impassable roads. In some metropolitan areas, wooden rails were installed on transportation corridors, and the ride across town became a pleasant experience rather than a bone-crunching, hold-on-for-your-life, mud-drenched experience. In many areas, a chapter was taken out of the Roman past, and roads of rock were laid down, and like those in Kusadasi you could, over time, see the tracks, worn into the rock by the passage of millions of iron wheels.

By the end of the century, the population had grown to over three hundred and sixty million and the level of scientific, cultural, and political advancement and sophistication was well beyond the point where earth would be in the tenth or twelfth century. The added brain trust was showing it's worth, and while there were no imposing castles and Goliath churches dotting the countryside, there were happy and productive people with a zest for the future, where invention and innovation where the primary motivators.

They did celebrate the birth of their spiritual and mortal leader at Christmas time as well as the changing of the seasons at the spring and the fall equinox, but Palm Sunday, Good Friday, Easter, and all the death-related holidays were unknown to the peoples of Teren as was the bible. The *God's Laws* book had wide circulation and was used as the basis for settling civil matters, but then altercations, and civil strife were extremely rare occurrences. There were very few lawyers as most of life on Teren was based solidly on the Golden Rule.

Wars: None

7

Earth: 600 to 799

I n the 600s, the new Islamic Empire which came out of the Arabian Peninsula defeated both the Roman and Pantheon empires. During these tumultuous times, the Quran (610) became Islam's handbook, and the crusades that would come to a peak, over the next few centuries, would be organized by the Western European Christians to repel the *Muslim wars of expansion. Their objective would be to retake control of the Holy Lands, reconquer pagan areas, and recapture formerly Christian territories.

On the site of Solomon's Temple, in Jerusalem, Omar the Great built an impressive mosque in 637, and the Saracens claimed the Holy Lands. Fear spread throughout Europe like the plague as the Muslim aggression seemed unstoppable. In towns like Ronda, Spain, the Christians were tortured and killed by the Islamic invaders, and their diabolical instruments of death can be viewed today at the

---

* and to Mr. Obama who said that the Crusades were as bad as any of the wars the Muslims instigated, I ask: "What part of defense don't you understand? The Christian Crusades were only taking back what the Muslims had taken by war. Go to Ronda, Spain, Mr. exPresident and see the instruments of torture that the Muslims used on Christians. But, of course, anyone who thinks the Muslim call to morning prayer is the most beautiful thing in the world would not be moved by millions of Christian dying at Muslim hands. Just look at what ISIS has done in Syria and Iraq in the last six years, with virtually no response." (Liberal readers may find this paragraph offensive, but the truth is the truth.)

Catholic church in the middle of the city (a sobering reminder of the brutality of the invaders, not unlike what is going on in Syria and Iraq today with the ISIS butchers.)

Finally, in 732, at the Battle of Tours, the Spanish Moors were sent packing from Gaul, never to return in such force. The Christian leader was Charles Martel, and the battle took place near Poitiers, France. Victory at Tours ensured the ruling dynasty of Martel's family or, as they were called, the Carolingians. Charles's son Pepin became the first Carolingian king of the Franks, and his grandson Charlemagne carved out a vast empire which covered Western Europe and beyond.

Charlemagne was also known as Charles the Great or Charles I (King of the Franks), and under his leadership, Europe was protected from the Muslim invaders. His actions laid the foundations for modern France, Germany, and the low countries. He took the Frankish throne in 768 and became King of Italy in 774, and from 800 to his death in 814, he was the first holy Roman emperor—the first such since the fall of the Roman Empire three centuries earlier.

Charlemagne has been called the "Father of Europe," and his rule spurred the Carolingian Renaissance, a period of energetic cultural and intellectual activity within the Western church. There was seldom a time that he was not at war, often at the head of his elite Seara bodyguard squadrons, with his legendary sword Joyeuse. In the Saxon Wars, spanning thirty years and eighteen battles, he conquered Saxonia and proceeded to convert those conquered to Christianity.

Charlemagne's death greatly affected many of his subjects, particularly those of the literary clique who had surrounded him in his later years—an anonymous monk lamented.

"From the lands where the sun rises to western shores people are crying and wailing the Franks, the Romans and all Christians, are stung with mourning and great worry…the young and old, glorious nobles, all lament the loss of their Caesar…the world laments the death of Charles…0 Christ, you who govern the heavenly host grant a peaceful place to Charles in your kingdom…"

Charlemagne must be turning over in his grave as the current German government allows unvetted immigration of tens of thousands, if not hundreds of thousands of undocumented Muslims, most of whom are young men. What the Muslims could not accomplish by military means in 732 may be coming to pass, in the twenty-first century, and Germany and for that matter, all of Europe may one day become Muslim nations rather than Christian nations.

In Asia, the porcelain technology (700) evoked an obsession with fine arts, cultural development, and refinement. The Chinese capital of Chengqiang (now Xi'an) is now the world's largest city. It covers thirty square miles, has a population of over one million, and is surrounded by an imposing wall. Under the rule of Emperor Xuanzong (713–756), it was a classical period devoted to literature, pottery, music, and calligraphy. In 751, however, at the battle of Talas, fought against the Arab Abbasid Empire, over control of the Syr Darya river area, the Chinese lost a great deal of influence in Central Asia. The emerging Abbasid Caliphate was the third of the Islamic caliphates to succeed the Islamic prophet Muhammad, and in 750, it ruled over a large and flourishing empire from its capital in Baghdad. For the next three centuries, the empire consolidated Islamic rule and cultivated great intellectual and cultural developments throughout the Middle East. This period became known as the Golden Age of Islam.

In South America, the Olmec people built big stone temples at Tenochtitlan and other Olmec cities (modern Mexico). In Central America (Guatemala), the Maya built temples between 250 B.C. and 900 A.D., and further south, in the Moche kingdom (Peru), more large stone buildings were constructed. The Inca conquered most of the Pacific coast of South America (Peru and Ecuador), and they too built large stone buildings and temples; most famous of these are the Pyramid of the Sun and the Pyramid of the Moon.

In North Africa, including Egypt, the Arab armies conquered the surrounding areas and made them part of the vast Islamic caliphate. Meanwhile, in the Nubian kingdoms, located in the Upper Nile Valley, the people embraced the Christian religion and had a vibrant culture in place. In West Africa, the powerful and wealthy kingdom of Ghana came into prominence, built on the proceeds from the lucrative trans-Saharan trade in salt, gold, and slaves.

Meanwhile, on the island of Madagascar, one of the most remarkable migrations in world history has been completed with the arrival of boat-borne colonists from South East Asia. About the same time, groups of Bantu made the crossing from East Africa to homestead in Northern Madagascar.

The population of the earth is now pegged at around two hundred and twenty-six million, and numerous wars that took place, all over the planet, killed millions upon millions. These wars include the following: Byzantine–Sasanian (602–608), transition from Sui to Tang (628), Jewish revolt (614), Second Perso–Turkic War (619), Muslim–Quraysh (622), Third Perso–Turkic War (627), First Caracol–Naranjo (627), Second Caracol–Naranjo (628), Emperor Taizong's Tujhe campaign (629–630), Battle of Hunayn (630), Third Caracol–Naranjo (631), Ridda Wars (632), Muslim conquest of Persia (633–644), Muslim conquest of Levant (634–638), Fourth Caracol–Naranjo (636), Muslim conquest of the Maghreb (637–709), Taizong's campaign against Tuyuhun (634–635), Tibetan attack on Songzhou (638), Muslim conquest of Egypt (639–642), Tang campaigns against the Western Turks (640–657), Tang campaign against Karakhoja (640), Tang against Karasahr (644), Goguryeo–Tang (644–668), Tang campaign against Kucha (648), Taizong's campaign against Xueyantuo (645–646), Second Tikal–Calakmui (650–695), First Fitna (656–661), Tikal–Dlos Pilas (657–672), Baekje–Tang War (660–663), Silla–Tang Wars (670–676), Jinshin War (672), Byzantine–Bulgarian (680–1355), Second Fitna (680–692), Palenque–Tonina Wars (687–711), Battle of Varnakert (702), Umayyad conquest of Hispania (711–718), Frankish Civil War (715–718), Siege of Constantinople (717–718), Islamic invasion of Gaul (719–759), Hayato Rebellion (720–721), Third Tikal–Calakmul (720–744), Battle of Tours (732), Muhammad invasion of Georgia (735–737), Berber Revolt (739), Zaydi Revolt (740), Conquest of Waka (743), Conquest of Naranjo (744), Abbasid Revolution (746–750), Battle of Talas (751), An Lushan Rebellion in China (755–763) which is reported to have killed thirty-six billion people. The Jinshin War (762–763), Alid Revolt (762–763), Fujiwara no Nakamaro Rebellion (764), Saxon Wars (772–804), Battle of

Bagrevand (775), Rebellion of Elpidius (781), Battle of Fakhkh (786), Qaysi–Yamani war (793–796), Viking Raids on British Isles (793–850), Viking Invasion of Ireland (795–902), Viking invasion of Francia (795–940).

Recorded wars: Sixty-one

8

Teren: 600 to 799

In the year 102, on planet earth, a scientist named Heron Alexandrines, who lived in Egypt, invented the aeolipile (wind ball). It was a simple bronze sphere that was positioned in such a way that it could rotate around its axis. From *L*-shaped nozzles that are opposite each other, steam exits, resulting in torque which causes the sphere to spin. The steam was created by boiling water either inside the sphere or under it. If the boiler was under the sphere, it was connected to the rotating sphere through a pair of pipes that serve as pivots for the sphere. It operated somewhat like the exhaust of today's jet engine. (Replicas of the Heron machine have been clocked at 1,500 rpm.)

If Heron had taken his invention just one tiny step further by envisioning uses for the mechanical power he had created the industrial revolution, on earth, may have been advanced by 1500 years.

Unfortunately, earthlings had to wait until 1781 before James Watt would patent a steam engine that produced continuous rotary motion; however, on Teren, the aeolipile principal led to the creation of a steam-operated water pump by scientists in 625. Shortly thereafter, a steam-powered piston/cylinder arrangement provided horsepower for almost any application from thrashing machines to paddle boats. The industrial revolution accelerated at warp speed, and by 675, high-grade kerosene was powering a piston/cylinder-type internal combustion engine that would allow man, someday, to fly over the moon and beyond, as Jesus had so cleverly speculated.

From 700 to 799, advancements on Teren rivaled those that went on earth between 1800s and 1900s. Airplanes were filling the skies, automobiles and trains were speeding people and goods around the planet, and ships no longer had to wait for the wind. Electricity and all its benefits were being explored, and dams and hydroelectric installations were installed on almost every river on the planet.

The dams not only provided electricity but also controlled the wild rivers which stopped the annual flooding which had been a part of life since the beginning of time.

Petrochemical products, communications equipment, photography, medical advancements like the X-ray, and all manner of diagnostic equipment were coming on line daily, and the standard of living, in every country, was exceeding anything the peoples of the planet had ever contemplated. The pace of the advancements, the scope and the sheer volume were truly amazing. As God, and the earth Jesus, looked down from heaven, they were impressed with the creativity their humans were showing, and when they discussed the difference, between what was going on in earth and Teren, they were somewhat perplexed.

God: It amazes me that earthlings have such a fascination with war and with all the war-related paraphernalia.

Jesus: Yes, it seems like acquiring territory and killing your neighbor because they do not look like you or talk like you or worship like you is high on their priority list. Why do you think that is, Father?

God: It may be the influence of the devil or it could just be the lack of central authority. Everyone on Teren knows your brother is the son of God and that the laws he espouses are my laws and breaking those laws have consequences so everyone follow the rules. There are no locks in Teren, every door is open and yet no one steals, no one does harm to a neighbor, because the son of God is living among them.

Jesus: Do you think that earthlings would change if I returned there to live and teach?

God: Yes, but then, we would deprive the humans on earth the opportunity to solve their problems by their own volition. It could be that they will see the light and control their own destiny or they may very well blow the planet to smithereens with weapons of mass destruction, which they will someday develop.

Jesus: Do you think my brother would like a break? I would be glad to take his place for a while. It might be a pleasant interlude for both of us?

God, looking down his nose over his gold rimmed glasses and with a calculating smile on his weathered face, replied, "I'll think about that son. Yes, I'll think about that…"

Teren population: 414 million

Wars: None

9

Earth: 800 to 999

By 800, the earth's population was just below 290 million while Teren's population had ballooned to around four hundred and fourteen million. Thus, earth had one hundred and twenty-four million less brains, and of those, at least half were either engaged in thinking about building fortresses, castles, and gigantic churches or were emerged in the quest to control neighbors and their lands. Great armies roamed the valleys and plains bringing death and destruction wherever they went. Vast resources both human and gold were expended on the tools of war and on feeding the armies. As a result, scientific advancements came slow, and the average peasant saw little change from generation to generation.

The dark ages (500 to 1000 A.D.), as they were known, was partly because many aspects of the Roman civilization were lost.

Feudalism in these times was a period of intense invasions that disrupted life in Europe and completely destroyed the former great Carolingian Empire of the Franks. The nobles, knights, and kings fought the wars; the church priests, bishops, and monks prayed; and the peasants (serfs) were the workers who performed the work to maintain the lord's manor lands. In addition, the serfs paid taxes not only to the lord but also to the church. They rarely left the manor, because the manor was self-sufficient; producing almost everything one needed for daily life. The serfs accepted their economic hardships, because they were taught by the church and believed that God "determined" a person's social position before they were born. To leave the community in which they were born would be questioning God's wisdom, and it was a sin to question the church.

The feudalism of Europe was in many ways similar to what was going on in Japan. Similarities were that both systems were grounded in political values that all participants seemed to embrace. Mutual ties and obligations were strong with many institutions and rituals expressing them. It was also highly militaristic with such values as physical courage, family alliances, loyalty, and ritualized combat highly prized. Both systems also showed aggressive contempt for non-warriors. The primary difference between the Japanese and European systems was that the feudalistic ties relied on group and individual loyalties whereas it was a more formal arrangement in Europe where ties were sealed by negotiated contracts, with explicit assurances given to the participants as to the advantages of the contract.

In the Arab wars with the Byzantine Empire, the conflicts had settled down into border skirmishing, with Arabs raiding deep into Anatolia (current-day Turkey) to capture booty and to force Christians to be their slaves, throughout the Abbasid Caliphate. The Caliph Al-Ma'mun in an effort to bring down the level of wars of retaliation gathered scholars of many religions to Baghdad with the intent of translating many of the Greek philosophy and scientific works. As part of this peace effort, he received from the Byzantine Emperor a number of Greek manuscripts annually, one of these being Ptolemy's astronomical work, the Almagest. Al-Ma'mun was enchanted with Ptolemy's work and used it as a base to establish astronomical operations in the plains of Mesopotamia. The crater Almanon on the moon is named in recognition of his contributions to astronomy.

Caliph Al-Ma'mum was a pioneer of cartography, having commissioned a world map from a large group of astronomers and geographers. The map shows large parts of the Eurasian and African continents with recognizable coastlines and major seas. It depicts the world as it was known to the captains of the Arab sailing ships (dhows) who used the monsoon wind cycles to trade over vast distances. By the ninth century, Arab sea traders had reached Guangzhou, China, and everywhere in-between.

One of Europe's most important events happened in August of 843 with the signing of the Treaty of Verdun which partitioned the Carolingian Empire among the three surviving sons of Emperor Louis I or, as he was known, Pious. The treaty was the first stage in the dissolution of the empire of Charlemagne and foreshadowed the formation of the modern countries of Western Europe.

In northern Europe the period between 800 and 1050 is generally considered the Viking age. There were Danish, Swedish, and Norwegian Vikings, and they ranged far and wide, spreading their brand of death and destruction. Danish Vikings worked down the European coast and ventured into England and Ireland. They also sailed down the French coast, around Portugal and Spain, through the Gibraltar Straight and into the Mediterranean Sea.

The Swedish Vikings explored the Baltic region and sailed up the rivers that empty into the Baltic Sea. They also sailed the Volga Rivers as far as the Black Sea and Constantinople. The Norwegian Viking, Leif the Happy, led a trip from Brattahlid (Greenland) that went on as far as Wineland, the east coast of today's America, and thus became the first Europeans to discover the North American continent.

Meanwhile, in the scientific world, the tidal mill gave the farmer some power to supplement back breaking human power. As the tide came in, it entered a millpond through a one-way gate. When the tide receded, the trapped water was released to turn a water wheel. One of the earliest tide mills was found on the island of Strangford Lough in Northern Ireland. The millstone, the receding water turned was 830 mm (33 inches) in diameter and was estimated to have developed 7/8 hp.

In China, the "fire lance" was developed by the Song dynasty. It was a bamboo tube that used gunpowder to propel shrapnel. It was thus the first weapon to use gunpowder. The Chinese had been making rockets for decades using a mixture of sulfur, charcoal, and potassium nitrate. The technology would not come to the rest of the world until the thirteenth century.

In India, the concept of zero as a number, and not merely a symbol for separation, was being put forth, and the world soon embraced this new concept. India also made advances in iron working as architects begin using iron beams to replace wooden beams for building large temples. About the same time, the Indian textile industry invented the churka, a wooden machine that used new kinds of gears to get the seeds out of cotton more efficiently.

Around 975, the Europeans started the conversion from Roman numerals to Arabic numbers and merged the Indian concept of zero into the mix. Paper money was developed in China, and the world soon followed their lead.

In the Americas, Tula, the largest city in Mexico, covered five square miles and had a population of about sixty thousand. At its center, the sacred precinct features two large ballcourts and two stepped pyramids which were decorated with carved panels showing feathered serpents, prowling jaguars, coyotes, and eagles with a human heart in their talons. The Maya city states, in the central regions, started to decline during the tenth century, and this vacuum brought the northern and southern regions into prominence. In Yucatan, Chichen Itza falls to be replaced by Mayapan as the dominant center. In the Guatemalan highlands, to the south, the K'iche' warrior people from the Gulf Coast established a modest tribute state. Art is produced primarily for deity worship and religious ritual rather than for use by divine warriors and gods.

Further north, the Mississippian culture spread out over the North American landscape, starting about 800 and flourished until the early 1600s. This Native American civilization was composed of a series of urban settlements and satellite villages linked together by a loose trading network, with the largest city being Cahokia. (Located across the Mississippi River from modern-day St. Louis, it had a population of over twenty thousand, and the city encompassed at least one hundred and twenty mounds.)

A number of cultural traits are recognized as being characteristic of the Mississippians. Most built large truncated earthwork pyramids, mounds, or platform mounds. These were usually square but could be rectangular or occasionally circular. Structures or burial buildings were usually constructed atop such mounds. The society was a maize-based agriculture one that developed all manner of pottery and cooking-based implements. Trade was widespread with networks extending as far west as the Rockies, north to the Great Lakes, south to the Gulf of Mexico, and east to the Atlantic Ocean.

As usual, wars raged all over the planet: Khan Krum's War (807–814), Paphlagonian expedition of the Rus' (830), Sweet Dew Incident (835), Era of Fragmentation (842–1247), Viking Raids in Spain (844), Viking Raid in Portugal (844), Rus'–Byzantine War (860), Hungarian invasions of Europe (862–973), Viking Invasion and Occupation of the British Isles (865–954), Zanj Rebellion (869–883), Battle of Bathys Ryax (872), Frankish–Moravian War (882–884), Byzantine–Bulgarian War (913), Rus'-Byzantine War (907), Caspian Expedition of the Rus' (913), Second Viking Invasion of Ireland (914–980), Battle of Sevan (924), Battle of Lenzen (929), Battle of Bach Dang (938).

Rebellion of Bordas Phokas the Younger (987–989), Tengyo no Ran Japan (940), Rus'–Byzantine War (941), Caspian Expedition of Rus' (943), Battle of Lechfeld (955), Destruction of Khazaria (965–969), Second Viking Raid in Portugal (966), Sviatoslav's invasion of Bulgaria (967–971), Byzantine conquest of Bulgaria (968 –1018), War of Three Henries (977–978), Second Viking Invasion of the British Isles (960–1012), First conflict Goryeo–Khitan War (993), Peasants' revolt in Normandy (996), Koppany's Revolt (Hungary) (996), Battle of Svolder (999), and Leinster revolt against Brian Boru (Dublin) (999).[*]

Recorded wars: Thirty-five

---

[*] Walter M. Montano, a former Catholic priest, asserts in his book, *Behind the Purple Curtain* that as many as fifty million people died for their Christian faith during the one thousand and two hundred years of the Dark Ages.

10

Teren: 800 to 999

In year 811, the first real rockets made their debut on planet Teren, other than the fireworks models that the Chinese had been firing off for centuries. At first, they were just interesting experiments, but as more powerful and larger units were developed and became more sophisticated, the astronomers running the programs were convinced that a rocket could be built that could go to the moon. If it was possible to place a payload (like a telescope) on the moon, where observations could be made without the interference of the planet's atmosphere, then they would have made a giant stride toward understanding more about the solar system and the stars beyond. Working with electronics similar to what earth had in the 1960s, it was a real challenge and some of the earliest attempts actually put spent rockets in orbit around the earth, and that sparked a wave of enthusiasm, throughout the scientific community, that was infectious.

It was not a quantum leap to envision a spacecraft that could take humans for a ride around the planet and maybe beyond. By 895, just eighty-four years later, astronauts were flying themselves into orbit, landing on the moon and returning in a reusable rocket (similar to the space shuttle) that they named Pegasus, after the flying horse of Greek mythology. (Pegasos or Pegasus was the immortal, winged horse which sprang from the neck of the beheaded Gorgon Medousa (Medusa). It was tamed by Bellerophon who rode it into battle against the fire-breathing monster known as the Khimaira (chimera). Later, the hero was attempting to fly to heaven, but Zeus caused the horse to buck, throwing Bellerophon back down to earth in disgrace. Pegasos winged his way on to Olympus where he became the thunderbolt-bearer of Zeus).

During the last quarter of the century, scientists in Japan were experimenting with a way to miniaturize electronics, and after almost forty years of research and development, with some of the planet's finest brains contributing to the project, a penetrating light-ray machine was developed using X-rays and gamma rays combined with what they named GC-rays. The GC-rays were captured by radio telescopes from a minus-one magnitude star (minus one is the value assigned to the brightness star in the night time sky) of the Globular Cluster type which consists of many old stars packed tightly together in spherical form. This globular cluster when viewed through telescopes looked like a hazy grouping of mothballs, and it put out the GC-rays in a steady unending stream.

Through a series of highly intricate and complicated maneuvers designed to combine the properties of the three different beams, the scientists were able to build a machine that emitted a penetrating beam that would reduce the size of any object it impacted by almost ninety-five percent. It was the talk of the scientific world, and while it had major impact on miniaturizing parts for the electronic industries, there seemed to be no other worthwhile applications; however, a clever group of Chinese, mammologists experimenting with small animals discovered that the ray would turn a normal house cat into a creature the size of a very small mouse, and there seemed to be no adverse effect to the animals. The little creatures ran and jumped and reproduced with abandonment, and all manner of animals from horses to penguins were subjected to the procedure, and none showed any ill effects. One of the Chinese scientists, recently diagnosed with terminal cancer, decided he would zap himself, and just days before his anticipated demise he did just that. The staff found him on the floor of the processing chamber, a total functioning human being, three inches tall and weighing just seven pounds. One of the staff members put his hand on the floor and the "little man" hopped on and was lifted to the countertop for closer observation.

"Can you hear me?" one of the staff asked, and covering his ears, he nodded "yes," indicating with a finger to his lips that they needed to speak in hushed voices so as not to break his ear drums. For over an hour, the little man's teammates questioned him, and as far as anyone could tell, he had the same brain power as before, and he was not indicating or showing any discomfort or harmful effects from the transformation process.

Six months later, he was still alive and while he was too small to be examined, he appeared to have overcome the cancer and was functioning as a valuable part of his scientific team. The staff zapped his clothes and personnel gear, and he seemed to enjoy life in the cardboard box that the staff had converted into a home, for him, right there on the lab counter. His wife came to see him every day, and after much thought and conversation, they requested that the team zap her as well. The director of the research center was not enthused about the idea, but the pleadings from the "little man" and his wife finally won him over, and the entire staff was present at the "zapping" ceremony.

The conversion was a total success, and to celebrate the event, one of the staff built a miniature house, and it was installed in a garden setting on the lab counter. The couple seemed happy and contented, and nine months later, a third small person appeared on the planet. With magnifying glasses, the staff was able to examine the new arrival, which appeared normal in all respects, and the proud parents were ecstatic.

During the goings-on at the lab, over the last year and a half, the scientific team had put out a call to the scientists of the world asking for help to find a counter measure that would reverse the process, and shortly after the birth of the little man's daughter, scientists from Australia claimed that they had found the solution. In their down-under lab, all manner of animals had been reduced in size with the *GC*-ray technology and then returned to their original size with a combination of natural occurring herbal treatments mixed with a microwave/*GC*-ray combination.

The Chinese team experimented with the new reversal technology on all manner of life, and there seemed to be no downside to the procedure. The director of the lab asked the little couple if they would like to revert to their original size, and the world watched and waited as the process was applied to the "little man," along with his wife and baby. The procedure was a total success, and on examination, by a group of leading doctors, the family was declared in excellent health and "little man," as he was now called by his coworkers, showed no signs of cancer. Health experts around the world started experimenting with the procedure, and the scientific journals were reporting that the success rate against cancer was one hundred percent. In fact, no one diagnosed with cancer, that had been subjected to the size-reduction process, showed any signs of the dreaded disease once there were returned to their normal size.

By the late 900s every medical clinic in the world had the technology, and cancer, while still being diagnosed, was one hundred percent curable. The population of Teren, with no deaths from cancer, war, and crime jumped by staggering proportions, and by the year 1000, it was almost triple that of earth or nearly eight hundred million.

New agriculture lands were coming on line all over the planet, but demand was closing in on output levels, and the thinkers of the world were concerned that there could be a food crisis in the centuries to come. Agriculture experts and other scientists set out, with great resolve, to solve the problem. The people in China who had experience with "little man" put forth the idea that if all humans were reduced to "little man" size the food supply currently available would be adequate for centuries, maybe even millenniums to come. Others, around the planet, had equally out-of-the-box thinking, but none of the solutions seemed adequate, and during one of the high-council meetings in Jerusalem, Jesus observed, "I once ask if mankind would ever be able to sail over the moon like ships sail over the horizon, and that idea became reality. I have often wondered if there are other planets that could support human life?"

The question sparked beelike activity all over the planet but especially in the astronomical community. The rocket scientists had been building bigger and bigger rockets that would allow them to put large payloads into orbit, but there were physical limitations on the size of the rockets that could be built, and most felt, that they had reached that point. One brilliant scientists in Russia pointed out to his fellow team members, "If we reduced the size and weight of our payloads and the astronauts, with the *GC*-ray reduction technology, then the rockets we have would be more than adequate. I have been doing calculations and our biggest rocket, the Pluto VII which can carry a ninety-thousand-pound payload to the moon would be able to transport, in one trip, not only the reduction and the reverse machinery, but ten thousand reduced-size people and all their supplies and equipment needed to establish a new colony on any planet that had a suitable atmosphere."

The plan was put forth at the first quarterly meeting in the year 998, in Jerusalem, and with smiling approval from Jesus, and the high council, the expedition to populate the stars was given high priority, and the planning and coordination would be spearheaded by the world-renown Nationwide Aviation and Space Administration installation outside present-day Baghdad. The other planets in Teren's solar system had been ruled out as possible colonizing sites for being either too cold or too warm (similar to Mars and Venus). The search outside their own solar system was considered paramount, and teams of explorers, in the "little man" format, where fired off on a regular basis all during the first ten years of the new millennium.

In 1001, a news report form NASA sent the scientific world into high orbit. The article, blasted around the world on the Terens World Wide Net (TWWN), read, in parts, as follows:

"A newly discovered, roughly Teren-sized planet orbiting our nearest neighboring star might be habitable according to a team of astronomers using the European Southern Observatory's 3. 6 meter telescope at La Silla, Chile, along with other telescopes around the world. The exoplanet is at a distance from its star that allows temperatures mild enough for liquid water to pool on its surface."

"NASA congratulates ESO on the discovery of this intriguing planet that has captured the hopes and the imagination of the world," says a spokesman from NASA worldwide headquarters outside Baghdad. The new planet circles Proxima Centauri, the smallest member of a triple star system known to science fiction fans everywhere as Alpha Centauri. Just over four light-years away, Proxima is the closet star to Teren, besides our own sun.

The scientific discovery team has determined that the new planet, dubbed Alpha, is at least 1.3 times the mass of Teren. It orbits its star far more closely than Teren orbits its sun, taking only two hundred and ten days to complete a single orbit. Despite the unknowns, the discovery was hailed by NASA exoplanet hunters as a major milestone on the road to finding other possible life-bearing worlds within our stellar neighborhood.

God, looking down on the colonizing attempts, was pleased and nudged and repositioned several planets into orbits that would replicate Teren's relationship to its sun. He also helped guide the explorers through the cosmos, and in due time, stars, with planets circling them, that fit the criteria, were being cataloged and mapped by the tiny explorers from Teren, for future colonization.

God smiled to himself and said out loud, "Five hundred million more brains definitely make a difference."

Wars: None
Population: Eight hundred million

11

Earth: 1000 to 1199

The human suffering during the two hundred years between 1000 and 1200 was as great as any other time in human history. Millions upon millions of lives were lost in the wars that raged all over the planet.

These wars inlcue the following: Hungarian–Ahtum War (1008), Pesh War (1009), Second conflict in the Goryeo–Khitan War (1010–1011), Battle of Clontarf (1014), Cnut the Great's conquest of England (1015–1016), Kievan Succession (1018), Kleidion War (1014), Cannae War (1018), Chola expedition to North India (1019–1024), Chola invasion of Srivjaya (1025), Guray War (1025), Battle of Stiklestad (1030), Stefan Vojislav's Uprising (1035–1042), Peter Delyan Uprising (1040–1041), Rus'–Byzantine War (1043), Vata pagan uprising (1046), Former Nine Years War (1051–1063), Koppan War (1052), Baghdad falls to Seljuk Turks (1055), War of Three Sanchos (1065–1067), Battle of Stamford Bridge (1066), Norman conquest of England (1066–1088), Kiev uprising (1068–1069), Georgi Voiteh Uprising (1072–1073), Saxon Rebellion (1073–1075), Georgian–Seljuk Wars (1074–1203), Revolt of the Earls (1075), Varendra Rebellion (1075–1082), Great Saxon Revolt (1077–1088), Gosannen War (1083), Rebellion of 1088 (1088), First Crusade (1096–1099) Chola invasion of Kalinga (1097), Crusade of 1101 (1101), Chola invasion of Kalinga (1110), Balearic Islands expedition (part of the Crusades) (1113–1115), Venetian

Crusade (1122–1124), Byzantine–Hungarian War (1127–1129), Jurchen Campaigns against Song dynasty (1125–1208), Civil War Norway (1130–1240), The Anarchy (1135–1154), Battle of Heiji Era (1160) and (1185), Baussenque Wars (1142–1162), Second Crusade (1145–1149), Northern Crusades (1147–1242), Japanese Battle of the Hogen Era (1156), Norman invasion of Ireland (1169–1175), Revolt of 1173–1174, Battle of Montgisard (1177), Battle of Jacob's Ford (1179), Genpei War (1180–1185), Uprising of Asen and Peter (1185–1204), Muslims under Saladin retake Jerusalem (1187), Third Crusade (1189–1192), Torain War (1191), Conquest of Cyprus (1191), and the Livonian Crusade, the Fourth (1198–1290).

Millions of creative brains were never allowed to mature and realize their potential as young body after body fell on the bloody battlefields, from China and India throughout the Middle East and of course in every corner of Europe.

In Medieval Europe starting around 1050, the first agricultural revolution began with a shift to the northern lands. A mild climate change brought improved growing conditions between 700 and 1200, and this combined with the perfection of new farming devices spurred agriculture output. The heavy plow, three-field crop rotation, cloth-processing mills, paper-manufacturing, and many other innovations came on line with the increased use of horse power and the widespread use of iron. With an increase in agricultural advancements, Western towns and trade grow exponentially and Western Europe returned to a money-based economy.

In Asia, Murasaki Shikibu, a high-born Japanese lady-in-waiting writes the *Genji Monogatari (The Tale of Genji)*. This lengthy, poignant description of court life, romance, and intrigue, frequently interspersed with poetry, is often considered the world's first novel.

By 1057, in the Phoenix Hall of the Byodo Temple (in the Kyoto Prefecture) a gilded wooden statue of Amida Buddha was completed by the artist Jocho who was the greatest sculptor of the period. Jocho advanced the multiblock construction method (yosegi zukuri) which allowed the artist to create larger works. Previously, statues had been carved from single blocks of wood, and thus the size had been limited. Also, in Japan, the Buddhist monk Saigyo (1118–1190) compiles a threevolume collection of his own compositions, entitled *Sankashu* (The Mountain Hermitage). Saigyo's poems, which often have a melancholy tone, combine simplicity with deep emotion and evocative descriptions of nature, observed during the monk's several long journeys on foot around Japan. Here is an example:

> Let me die in spring under the
> blossoming trees, let it be around
> that full moon of Kisaragi month

In China, the Song (Sung) dynasty (960–1279) rules over what is often called "China's Golden Age." Enormous commercial growth, referred to by many historians as "pre-modern" in character distinguishes the period. The growth, mainly in nonagricultural goods, is led by silk which was the first true cottage industry, and by the production of cash, crops like tea that are sold, not consumed by the producer. As this commercial development took place, it led to the expansion of market forces into the daily lives of the ordinary people. During this period, the Chinese population grew enormously and the population center moved from the north of China (the wheat-growing area) to Hangzhou, below the Yangzi River (the rice-growing area), because the rice yield was higher per acre than wheat and could thus support a larger population. The Grand Canal which had been built during the Sui dynasty (581–619) connected the Yangzi and the Yellow rivers, and it facilitated the transport of agricultural production from the south to the north which helped unify China.

Meanwhile, in Europe, the reforming popes issued a decree in 1059 on papal elections which gave the cardinals the sole right to appoint new popes. This allowed papal elections to escape the whims of the current political leaders. Seven years later, William the Conqueror invaded England and at the Battle of Hastings, where thirty thousand men died, he established himself as the King of England and the Duke of Normandy. The language of England evolves into Middle English with English syntax and grammar but with a heavily French vocabulary. French art and literature prevailed, and the French language becomes the voice of the political realm. The stability William enjoys is in part to the feudal system he introduced which over the next two centuries progressed into a national monarchy the descendants of which rule England today.

In 1073, Gregory VII initiates a new conception of church. According to Gregory, the church is obligated to create "right order in the world," rather than withdraw from it. Gregory seeks to create a papal monarchy with power over the secular state and to establish ecclesiastical authority, thereby inauguration the "investiture controversy." Gregory excommunicates Henry IV in 1077, and this encourages the practice of Christian warfare in the pursuit of providing "right order in the world" and establishes religious enthusiasm in all of Christendom.

During the last years of the eleventh century and throughout the twelfth, 1095 through 1272, the Crusades were in full swing, and the loss of life, on both sides, will never be accurately known. The First Crusade captures Jerusalem, killing its Muslim inhabitants, and the slaughter continues through the Ninth Crusade which is commonly considered to be the last major medieval Crusade to the Holy Lands which took place in 1271–1272.

In 1165, the Frenchman Chretien de Troyes is the first writer to condense the legendary Arthurian history, based on the Celtic hero King Arthur and his knights of chivalry. Chretien is the first-known writer to put forth the idea of romantic love within marriage. His definition of chivalry includes the defense of honor, combat in tournaments, and the virtues of generosity and reverence. The noble code of chivalry is accompanied with the improvement in noble life and the status of noblewomen.

Muslims recaptured Jerusalem in 1187, and the Third Crusade is led by the German Emperor Frederick Barbarossa, the French King Philip Augustus, and the English King Richard the Lionhearted. There venture is not successful and that return home to lick their wounds and to mourn the thousands upon thousands they left dead on the Middle East battlefields. Two years later, in 1198, Innocent III is elected Pope, and he organizes the Fourth Crusade, with orders to capture Jerusalem from Islam control. The Fourth Crusade captures and sacks Constantinople with causes a firm and enduring hatred for the West by the Byzantine Islamic.

By 1200, earth's population is around three hundred and ninety-three million while Teren is pushing one thousand and five hundred billion. Over a billion more minds working on all man's fields of interest and activity from agriculture, arts, communications, travel, education, entertainment, family, government, politics, health, legal, monetary, financial affairs, professions, recreation, social, and of course religion. On Teren, the number of brilliant, Einstein-type minds, working for the collective good of humankind, is incalculable, whereas on earth, they seem to be far and few between as so many of the bodies, carrying such minds, met early deaths on unnamed battlefields, by club, lance, spear, ax, knife, or sword.

Recorded Wars: 55

12

Teren: 1000 to 1199

At the 1010 worldwide conference of territories and nations, held each decade in Jerusalem with the agenda established by Teren's CEO, i.e., Jesus, son of God, included only one primary topic. The bulletin transmitted to every iPad, smartphone, and computer in the world read in part as follows:

"The mission of the 1010 Jerusalem High Council meeting will be to come up with an all-inclusive long range plan that will solve the population problem for now and for a thousand years Into the future."

The almost twelve hundred people that attended the conference were the planets brightest and best minds and they represented a true cross section of Terens diverse population.

Jesus opened the meeting with a prayer and then said, "I once ask my followers to follow me and become fishers of men and I now ask you to follow your hearts and minds to find us a real and lasting solution for the overpopulation that many see coming. Planners estimate that by 1500 Terens population will be five times what it is today or over eight billion people and that will strain our ability to adequately feed everyone. No thinking is to radical and I urge you to explorer solutions that by today's standards may seem impossible. When you leave here in five days I hope that we will have a list of options that we can further study and refine."

The conference was divided into these six major areas of concern:

A. Birth control and health issues
B. Agriculture: new technology and trends
C. Cultivating the oceans vast resources
D. Colonization of other Teren like planets throughout the solar system.
E. Human-size reduction through compression system using the *GC*-ray technology.
F. Animal reduction using *GC*-ray compression technology.

The two hundred delegates to the birth control and health section were all doctors and medical experts, with a few theologians and educators mixed into the group. The eliminating of cancer, through the use of the *GC*-ray technology, had helped increase population levels, and the other chronic human diseases were being attacked with the same inquisitive vigor which would eventually increase population levels even further. The consensus of opinion was that the Hippocratic Oath was not adjustable and that the other subgroups would have to come up with their own solutions as the health industry could not stop their advancements that were having such a positive impact on the lives of the average person. There was one group, however, that presented a paper on birth-control methods that included giving female babies a vaccination at birth that would take twenty-five years to wear off, and during the twenty-five years, conception would be impossible. One of the groups scientists projected that this could reduce birth rates by up to fifteen percent. The collective minds decided to include the birth-control procedure in their final position paper. This, of course, would be acceptable in that the church, under Jesus's guidance and control, with direct authority form God, had never taken a position on birth control, unlike the Catholic Church on earth that had condemned any artificial means of contraception. (Jesus had put abortion on top of his priority list to discuss with his father on his next visit to heaven.)

The agriculture group drew from the farming community itself as well as the manufacturers of farm machinery and of course the educators and research fellows who had both feet firmly planted in the *terrafirma*. All manner of white papers were presented from reducing the height of rice stocks so monsoons would not knock down the plants during the growing season to the latest hydroponics, aeroponics, fogponics, and solution to culture advancements, which were all designed to grow plants without soil or soil-like media. All manner of creative growing and harvesting methods were explored, and much emphasis was given to automatic harvest methods that actually increased per-acre yields. As an example, olive, grape, and fruit tree orchards were being laid out and pruned so that harvest could be achieved by mechanical means and this automation also led to increase yields.

The ocean cultivation group made up of ocean farmers and scientists had been chartering a different course in recent years. Rather than relying on monolithic factory fish farms, these new ocean farmers were producing high-quality seafood in the form of seaweed, a nutrient-rich food source which is also a sponge for organic pollutants. One scientist from the Netherlands calculated that a global network of sea-vegetable farms totaling one hundred and eighty thousand square kilometers, roughly the size of Washington state, could provide enough protein for the entire world population. The real importance of these efforts is that ocean farming requires no fresh water, no deforestation, and no fertilizer, all significant downsides to land-based farming. Ocean farms would not be a total solution, but in the summary presented to the convention, the group stated unequivocally that ocean farms promise to be more sustainable than even the most environmentally sensitive traditional farms and that added food production from these facilities will be coming on line in the very near future. They lobbied that given worldwide recognition and priority sea farms could go a long way toward meeting the expanding population needs.

The colonization form was made up of some of the brightest and best minds Teren had to offer. From the planetariums and space centers around the world, including the NASA headquarters outside Baghdad, the colonizers were the most vocal and organized group, and all the members sported election type lapel buttons with a logo showing a space ship and the words, "Colonization, the only answer." Their position paper spelled out in detail the current efforts to locate Teren-like planets, and their search areas were taking their astronauts into deep space, thousands of light years away. The recent find, the planet dubbed Alpha circling our nearest sun, was pointed at with pride. Every scientists polled was certain that the latest probes would uncover more likely candidates, and that all Teren resources should be mobilized to search the billions of stars that the black sky displays every night. It was a bold argument, and when combined with the *GC*-ray technology and the new nuclear rockets that were currently being tested, it was a no brainier as far as the space scientists were concerned.

The *GC*-ray technology crowd was less vocal but totally convinced that downsizing the planets population was the easiest way to extend the planet's resources and to extend them indefinitely. The astronauts had proven that the little people could survive on just five percent of the normal-sized human calorie input, and if the planets population was so reduced, then current levels of food production would be adequate for thousands of years into the future. They further argued that current infrastructure could be better utilized if houses and apartment buildings were subdivided from the current average living area of two thousand square feet down to just a hundred square feet which would be more than adequate for the small-sized people. It was a compelling argument, but no one knew if Jesus and God would approve of such a dramatic change for humankind, although on the surface the argument had many positive aspects.

The last group, those advocating animal reduction using the *GC*-ray technology maintained that there would be no limit to the amount of protein-based food one could produce using their system. A beef producing steer weighting one thousand and four hundred pounds that consumes twenty-eight pounds of feed per day could be reduced to a seventy-pound animal eating just 1.4 pounds of feed per day. When the animal was mature, it could be returned to its original one-thousand-and-four-hundred-pound size prior to slaughter. This system, when applied to all animal-based food, could provide for the needs of billions, and the feed consumed would be just five percent of what is now required, thus taking pressure off the farmers that grow animal feed. In the paper, they presented to the convention it was noted that regardless of what other solutions might be instituted their system should be a requirement as there was no down size to their proposal, in fact numerous cattle, chicken, pig, mutton, and turkey farmers around the world were already making use of the *GC*-ray compression technology.

The conference came to a close with all parties proud of their input and with some upbeat prognoses for the future. One way or another, the population explosion would be addressed, and each group was satisfied that they had delivered the best solutions available.

Jesus and his council of elder men reviewed the position papers and were amazed at the original thinking that so many of the proposed solutions put forth.

Addressing the small group Jesus ask, "Is there any of the solutions that you could not embrace?"

Talmage, an older gentleman from Northern Ireland, replied, "I have no issue with any of the solutions except the reduction of the entire population of our planet into the small-sized people format. It is my humble opinion that your father made us in his image, and I really wonder if he would accept that from now on all life would be ninety-five percent smaller."

Smiling at Jesus, he continued, "Since I don't speak with him on a direct basis, and since you do maybe this is the one subject that you may wish to cover directly with our creator."

Jesus looking around his assembled colleagues and friends nodded and asked, "Do the rest of you share Talmage's assessment?"

There was unanimous consent and Jesus smiling continued, "I will therefore recommend that all the solutions put forth can be implemented, on a region by region basis, with the exception of downsizing everyone on the planet."

Heads around the conference table nodded in agreement. Jesus smiled and turning to his aid said, "Please draw up the proclamations and post them to all the citizens of Teren. Thank you for your contributions and the next worldwide conference will be in 1020, and I think we will look back and consider that the work done here has been truly monumental."

By 1210, just two hundred years later, a mere eyeblink for God and Jesus, Teren explorers had colonized two planets, one just fourteen light-years away and the other three light-years further in the same direction. The colonies started out as mere outposts in new world venues that for the most part were remarkably similar to Teren. Each outpost was manned by little people, but in some cases, their small size put them directly into the indigenous creatures food chain, so as soon as practical, the colonies reverted to normal human size and were thus able to better cope with the wild life on each planet.

The population of Teren had dropped from 1.5 billion back to eight hundred million with the new planets supporting about four hundred million each or about the same as earth's population would be in the 1500s.

The first planet colonized was called Teren-Alpha and the second, three light years further into the milky way, was named Teren-Beta. From time to time, Jesus would visit the new outposts and he was pleased to see that the people were following God's commandments even though the messenger was not there to act as a daily reminder. After centuries of practicing "do on to others," the human brand had come to realize the benefits of the Golden Rule and the Ten Commandments, and each venue operated as if Jesus was overseeing, and ever present, as he had been for centuries on Teren.

Wars: none

13

Earth: 1200 to 1399

In 1348 over 1.5 million Jews were killed in Europe on the suspicion that they (the Jews) had poisoned the water supply. As the Black Death Plague swept across Europe, it annihilated nearly half the population (some reports peg the deaths at seventy-five million), and Jews were made the scapegoats, likely because they seemed to be less affected than the rest of the population. The first massacres took place in April 1348 in Toulon, France, where the Jewish quarter was sacked and burned. Within the five hundred and ten Jewish communities destroyed, many members killed themselves to avoid the persecutions. One writer on the subject projected that "ordinary folk" hated the Jews, because they served the merchants and aristocrats and, with their loans and with their capital, helped establish urban economy and the city's governing political and territorial independence. Further, the Jews had exploited artisans with loans at usurious rates. These reasons gave the "ordinary folk" the motive to kill the Jews, because they were gaining political and social standing, while others saw the massacres as the "revenge of impoverished debtors against privileged elite of Jewish creditors."

During the two hundred years from 1200 to 1400 there were one hundred and twelve major wars or conflicts recorded on earth, and of course, this did not include the minor uprisings and skirmishes that never made it into the history books. The primary conflicts were as follows: War of the Antiochene Succession (1201), Fourth Crusade

(1202), Anglo Norman War (1202-04), Anglo French War (1202–1219), Bulgarian–Latin wars (1204–1261), Loon War (1206), Mongol invasions and conquests (1206–1337), Albigensian Crusade (1209–1229), Welsh uprising (1211), Fifth Crusade (1213–1221), Battle of Bouvines (1214), First Barons' War (1215–1217), Mongol conquest of the Qara Khitai (1216-18, War of the Succession of Champagne (1216-22), Sixth Crusade (1228-29), Friso–Drentic War (1230–1233), Dernbacher Feud (1230–1233), Bosnian Crusade (1235–1242), Livonian campaign against Rus' (1240–1242), First Prussian Uprising (1242–1249), War of the Flemish Succession (1244–1254), War of the Thuringian Succession (1247–1264), Genose occupation of Rhodes (1248–1250), Seventh Crusade (1248–1254), War of the Euboeote Succession (1256–1258), War of Saint Sabas (1256–1270), Rebellion of Arbanon (1257–1259), Toluid Civil War (1260–1264), Great Prussian Uprising (1260–1274), Mongol invasions of the Levant (1260–1323), Berke–Hulagu war (1262), Scottish–Norwegian War (1262–1266), Second Barons' War (1264–1267), Battle of Benevento (1266), Kaidu–Kublai war (1268–1301), Eighth Crusade (1270), Sambyeolcho Rebellion (1270–1273), Ninth Crusade (1271–1272), Manx revolt (1275), Uprising of Ivaylo (1277–1280), Conquest of Wales by Edward I (1277–1283), First Mongol invasion of Burma (1277–-1288), War of the Sicilian Vespers (1282–1302), War of the Limburg Succession (1283–1289), Battle of Red Ford (1294), Anglo–French War (1294–1303), Byzantine–Venetian War (1296–1302), First War of Scottish Independence (1296–1328), Franco Flemish War (1297–1305), Second Mongol invasion of Burma (1300–1301), Teutonic take-over of Danzig (1308), Siege of Puygitlaume (1308), Rebellion of mayor Albert (1311–1312), Dehli–Seuna War (1311–1318), Esen Buqa–Ayurbarwada war (1314–1318), Battle of Morgarten (1315), Bruce campaign in Ireland (1315 –1318), Swedish–Novgorodian Wars (1315–1318), Despenser War (1321–1322), Peasant revolt in Flanders (1323–1328), War of Metz (1324–1326), First War of the Rugen Succession (1326–1328), War of Hum (1326–1329), Polish– Teutonic War (1326–1332), Tver Uprising (1327), War of the Two Capitals (1328–1332), Serbian civil war (1331), Genko

War (1331–1333), Eltz Feud (1331–1337), Second War of Scottish Independence (1332–1357), Hundred Years' War (1337–1453), Galicia–Volhynia Wars (1340–1392), Bulgarian–Ottoman Wars (1340–1396), War of Breton Succession (1341–1364), Byzantine civil war (1341–1347), Battle of Zava (1342), Thuringian Counts' War (1342–1346), Second War of Rugen Succession (1342–1354), St. George's Night Uprising (1343–1346), Byzantine–Genoese War (1348–1349), Hook and Cod wars (1350–1490), Red Turban Rebellion (1351–1368), Byzantine civil war (1352–1357), Delhite invasion of Bengal (1353–1354), War of the Two Peters (1356–1375), Ispah Rebellion (1357–1366), Jacquerie Peasants' revolt (1358), Delhite invasion of Bengal (1358–1360), War of the Bands (1362–1457), Revolt of Saint Titus (1363–1368), Castilian Civil War (1366–1369), War of the Luneburg Succession (1370–1388), War of the Guelderian Succession, (1371–1379), Byzantine civil war (1373–1379), War of the Eight Saints (1375–1378), War of Chioggia (1378–1381), Tuchin Revolt (1378–1384), Battle of Kulikovo (1380), Peasants' Revolt England (1381), Lithuanian Civil War (1381–1384), Ming conquest of Yunnan (1381–1382), Harelle Peasants' revolt (1382), Despenser's Crusade (1382–1383), Greater Poland Civil War (1382–1385), Tokhtamysh–Timur war (1380–1390), Dohna Feud (1385), Forty Years' War (1385–1424), Timur's invasions of Georgia (1386–1404), War of the Cities (1387–1389), Epiphany Rising (1399–1400), and the Jingnan Campaign against Ming dynasty (1399–1402).

It is impossible to determine the number of lives that all of the above impacted, but it has to be in the millions maybe even as high as ten million. Earth's population starts out at about three hundred and ninet-three million in the year 1200, and two hundred years later, it is at four hundred and sixty-four million which represents an increase of just eighteen percent. In the same period, Teren's population doubled to about 2.2 billion.

During these stressful times (1200–1400), advancements were made, like the founding of the University of Paris, in 1200, by Phillip II, King of France, and of course the ever-present ecumenical council (number XIV) called by Alfonse III in 1274; the churches continuing effort to define and secure its leadership roll over the inhabitants of Europe. Westminster Abbey was built in 1220, and the tallest structure in the world, at one hundred and eighty-eight feet, was the Leaning Tower of Pisa that was completed in 1154.

In South America, the collapse of the Maya city states created a political vacuum in the central region. The northern and southern regions remained more viable, but they were strongly influenced by the central Mexican people. In Yucatan, Chichen Itza falls to be replaced by Mayapan as the dominant center and in the Guatemalan highlands the Kiche, a warrior people from the Mexican Gulf Coast, establish a modest tribute state. Art is produced primarily for deity worship and religious ritual rather than for use by the divine rulers. Warriors and gods, both local and Mexican, are frequent themes and only a few dated monuments are erected.

In the early thirteenth century, Mongol armies from North Asia gained control of Islamic territories, and by 1271 China, too, had succumbed to Mongol rule with the capital city relocated at Beijing.

A century later, Islamic power is restored in Central and West Asia under Timur, better known in the West as Tamerlane (1370–1405). Timur marries a Mongolian princess and establishes his rule in Central Asia and expands westward, gaining control over most of West Asia (parts of Iran, Iraq, Syria, and Anatolia) as well as parts of southern Russia and India. Bringing craftsmen from different conquered lands to his capital, Timur initiates one of the most brilliant and prolific periods in Islamic art.

In 1260, Khubilai Khan ascends to the Mongol throne and in 1264 moves the capital from Karakorum to Beijing. In 1271, he chooses the Chinese name Yuan for his dynasty, and by 1279, all of China has fallen under Mongol rule.

Meanwhile, back in Europe Wycliffe's Bible is the name now given to a group of Bible translations into Middle English that were made under the direction of John Wycliffe. They appeared over a period from 1382 to 1395 and were the chief inspiration and the main cause of the Lollard movement, a pre-Reformation movement that rejected many of the distinctive teachings of the Roman Catholic Church. In the early Middle Ages, most Western Christian people encountered the Bible only in the form of oral versions of scriptures, verses, and homilies in Latin (other sources were mystery plays, usually conducted in the vernacular, and popular iconography.) There are two distinct versions of Wycliffe's Bible that have been written. The earlier was translated during the life of Wycliffe, while the later version is regarded as the work of John Purvey. Since the printing press was not yet invented, there exists only a very few copies of Wycliffe's earlier Bible. The earlier Bible is a rigid and literal translation of the Latin Vulgate Bible, and Wycliffe's view of theology is closer to realism than to the spiritual. This version was translated word for word, which often led to confusion or meaninglessness. It was aimed toward the less learned clergymen and the laymen, while the second, more coherent versions was aimed toward all literates. The second version, though somewhat improved, still retained a number of infelicities of style, as in its version of Genesis 1:3.

Latin Vulgate: Dixitque Deus fiat lux eet facto est lux.

Early Wycliffe: And God seide, Be maad li3t; and li3t was maad

Later Wycliffe: And God seide. li3t be maad; and li3t was maad

Douay-Reims: And God said: Be light made. And light was made.

The familiar verse of John 3:16 is rendered in the later Wycliffe version as:

> Later Wycliffe: For God so louede so the world, that he 3af his oon bigetun sone, that ech man the bileueth in him perisch not, but haue everlasting life.
>
> King James Version: For God so loved the world, that he gave his only begotten Son, that whosoever believeth in him should not perish, but have everlasting life.

At this time, the Peasants' Revolt was running full force as the people of England united to rebel against the unfairness of the English Parliament and its favoring of the wealthier classes. The archbishop of Canterbury was able to turn both the church and parliament against

Wycliffe by falsely stating that his writings and his influence were fueling the peasants involved in the revolt. King Richard II ruled that Wycliffe be removed from Oxford and that all who preached or wrote against Catholicism be imprisoned. Later, after John Wycliffe died, the Council of Constance declared Wycliffe a heretic and under the ban, it was decreed that his books be burned and his remains be exhumed, burned, and cast into the River Swift.

Although Wycliffe's Bible circulated widely in the later Middle Ages, it had very little influence on the first English biblical translations of the reformation era. Due to the common use of surviving manuscripts of Wycliffe's Bibles as works of an unknown Catholic translator, this version continued to circulate among the sixteenth century English Catholics, and many of its renderings were adopted by the translators of the Rheims New Testament. Since the Rheims version was consulted by the translators for the King James Version, a number of reading from Wycliffe's Bible did find their way into the Authorized King James Version of the Bible.

The "Middle Ages," (500–1450) represented the time between the fall of Roman Empire and the revival of civilization starting with the European Renaissance. Starting about 1000, Europe showed signs of revitalizing, in great measure because of the Crusades. The Crusaders discovered sophisticated cultures to the east and incorporated many of the arts and advancements into their daily lives.

Before about 1300, Europe was populated by serfs, or peasants, who were tied to the lands owned by their particular nobility or ruling classes. These mini-kingdoms tended to be isolated from each other, and as a result, the serfs were trapped in their surroundings and tied to the land. The Catholic church enlisted wandering ministries to spread their brand of the word of God. The two primary orders were the Franciscans, known for their vows of poverty and ability to relate to peasants, and the Dominicans, a more scholarly order who ministered more to educational needs. The monasteries that spread all over Europe were retreats where the common man could find protection, where the church could maintain safe havens, and where scholarship and education could be advanced by the monks who were usually the only people in Europe who could read or write. Some of these monasteries eventually became the first European universities.

In the year 1327 over two hundred thousand Moors invaded Spain. The Moors were the Muslim inhabitants of the Maghreb, North Africa, the Iberian Peninsula, Sicily, and Malta. In the mid-1300s their Umayyad Caliphate collapsed which fragmented Islamic power on the Iberian Peninsula. Christian kingdoms in the north gradually united expanding their territories through a campaign of Reconquista (reconquest.) Despite the weakening of Islamic power, its influence in science, medicine, and art contributed to the rich diversity on the peninsula as Christians, Muslims, and Jews managed to live peacefully together. By 1399, the Christian kings conquered virtually all of Muslim al-Andalus leaving Granada and the surrounding territory as the last bastion of Islamic Iberia. (Granada covered a small strip of ground from the straights of Gibraltar up the Mediterranean coast west of Valencia.)

In 1308, cannons were first used by the French at the siege of Puyguitlaume and handheld cannons (culverin) were being experimented with in the Chinese territories. These inventions would bring war and killing on the blue planet to a whole new level.

Recorded wars: 112

14

Teren Alpha & Beta 1200 to 1399

Of the four hundred million Terenlings on Teren-Alphaa, three hundred and ninety million had arrived by nuclear rockets, in the little man format, and the balance were born on the new planet. Because the indigenous animal life was about twenty percent larger than most of the mammals found on Teren, it was quickly determined that the small man format would not do and the conversion machines worked thirty-two hours per day to get the population back to normal size. (Thirty-two hours because that is how long it took Alpha to rotate a full three hundred and sixty degrees.)

The planet had continents, oceans, rivers, deserts, forestlands, and floating cloud like islands that would have floated off into space except the trees, growing on each island, sent down long tentacle roots that held each such island firmly in place. Some of the floating islands were only a few feet above the planets base while others towered a thousand feet into the air. As the trees matured and their roots lengthened, the island would rise, only held in place by its root anchors. Below each of the islands, which could be as small as a football field or as large as several hundred acres, the ground was swamp-like. The sun never reached the areas below the floating islands, and as a result, each area under was almost void of undergrowth; more of a swamp-type depression which made the Terenlings wonder if at one time, each island had been a part of the mainland. From near space, the planet looked like a green tennis ball with fuzzy-like mushrooms randomly dotting the surface.

The creatures that had roamed and controlled the planet since its inception did not take kindly to a new life form, especially one that could direct a beam at them that would reduce their size by ninety-five percent. In a minute, the bear-like creature standing twenty feet tall could be reduced to koala size, and in no time the local animals were no longer a threat to the farmers working the newly cleared fields. The dairy and beef herds quickly adapted to their new surroundings and life on Alpha settled into Teren-like patterns. Roads, airfields, and structures of all kinds sprang up on the twelve land masses that formed the primary continents.

The weather was a few degrees cooler than Teren, and the mountaintops rarely peaked out from their snow coverings. The atmosphere was a bit thicker in that the clouds were denser, and instead of seventy-eight percent nitrogen and twenty-one percent oxygen, the atmosphere on Alpha was eighty-five percent nitrogen and twelve percent oxygen with three percent other gases like carbon dioxide, nitrous oxides, methane, and argon. The human body seemed to be able to cope with the difference with no apparent ill effects. Gravitation was the only real difference the Teren-Alpha people had to overcome in that gravity on Alpha was less than Teren by about twelve percent and the difference meant that a running man could actually become airborne and rain did not beat down but rather almost floated down like snowflakes. A glass that fell from a counter would not end up on the floor smashed but would more or less float to a soft landing. The ocean tides were small and non-eroding, and as a result, the beaches were more rock than sand. The sporting events of high jump and pole vaulting were at levels that earthlings or Terenlings could never hope to attain, and while the gravitational force was different, it presented no real impediment to progress on the fuzzy green planet.

On Teren-Beta life was an extremely challenging for the new arrivals who by 1400 numbered about two hundred million. The planet was smaller than Teren by about twenty percent, and it had a ring around it similar to the one that encompasses our Saturn. There were some forty large moons in the ring with the largest being twenty-five miles in diameter, and there were thousands of lesser moons from bowling-ball size to astrodome size with everything in-between. The ring casts a permeant lace-like shadow on the surface of the planet and moonlight was about a quarter of sunlight, so there was no part of the planet that ever got really dark.

The atmosphere was dense, similar to Teren-Alpha, and there were only four continents, each about the size of Europe and Asia combined, that were scattered along the equator, all many thousands of miles apart. The rest of the planet was a greenish-blue ocean that had tides that rose and fell, dramatically, with the movement of the moons that composed the ring above. The tide levels could rise and fall over one hundred feet along the coasts of all the continents, and the action was so intense that no one could live near the shore but the creative minds of the Beta-Terenlings harnessed the movement of the water with huge catchment basins that filled at high tide, and then as the ocean receded, the water was released from the basins, generating electricity as the water rushed past the turbines on its way back to the ocean. The ocean liners that were built had to stay miles away from shore and rely on smaller shuttle barges to ferry cargo and passengers back and forth using giant wharfs that could withstand the ocean surges. The liners were an extremely popular form of recreation in that they could sail directly under the ring and launch rocket type helicopters that could take people for day trips to the different moons. Each of the forty large moons had their own unique features. Some were covered in forests, some had mountains to climb, others had glasslike surfaces where all manner of fossils had been trapped in the glass as it had welled up from the interior of the mini planet. There was no end to the varied surfaces and eventually each moon was named and people kept journals on which ones they had visited. You were considered a top-notch traveler if your journal/passport showed that you had been on all forty of Beta's moons.

As the immigrants/explorers developed each continent under the oscillating lace-like shadows that came and went with the movement of the ring, they noticed that there was a fine white powder left on the leaves of their plants each time the ring passed overhead. This "ring dust" as it was called was analyzed in the university laboratories and found to contain high levels of a nitrogen-like element that had never been known before. Experiments where initiated all over the planet and showed that it would slow the aging process dramatically. Dust collection panels were developed, and within no time the Beta-Terenians were exporting "ring dust" pills back to Teren and to their neighbors on Alpha.

Back on Mother Teren, the press of population growth had been reduced dramatically by the departures to Alpha and Beta to almost seven hundred million people, which left the planet's population at a manageable number of around 1.2 billion. During the two hundred years between 1200 and 1400, Teren's technological advancements equaled and exceeded what on earth would take another nine hundred years to accomplish. As God and Jesus discussed the differences, they marveled at the stark difference between the technological advancements on the parallel planets. After analyzing all the available data, they could find no explanation for the vast differences other than millions of young, bright, inquisitive brains were not being left on blood-drenched battlefields as mulch or rat food.

Wars: None

15

Earth: 1400 to 1599

In 1400, the Mongol conqueror Tamerlane invaded Syria after devastating Georgia and Russia. The next year he laid waste to Aleppo, Damascus and Baghdad. In 1402, Tamerlane then went on to defeat the Ottoman sultan at the battle of Angora. Some reports say the two armies, at Angora comprised over three million men and you can only guess at the loss of life. The logistics of feeding and finding water for three million men and their animals must have been a full-time job for thousands upon thousands of the forces and it is assumed that the local populations went without so that the armies could be fed. The Timurid Army had about three dozen elephants, obtained during Tamerlane's raids into northern India in 1397–1398. The animals were equipped with armor and had large knives attached to their tusks. The horses on the opposing side were intimidated by the elephants size and smell, and this lead to wild clashes as the armies came together. If the elephants handler was knocked from his perch, the animal might well run wild and slash his way indiscriminately through friend and foe. It must have been a wild and confusing scene as the two armies engaged.

Much of the Timurid army was medium to heavy cavalry with the main weapons being the composite bow, lance, mace, and sword. The riders wore plated chain mail or metal lamellar armor (made from horizontal overlapping rows of small armor plates), and their horse wore leather or metal lamellar armor. Causality figures cannot be given because no one can be sure of the two armies actual size, but it would not be unusual to say that at least fifty percent of the Turkish army was killed, captured, or wounded and that the victorious army probably sustained causalities in the thirty percent range.

With such a complete victory, Tamerlane had the Ottoman Empire at his mercy. He guided his army to the shores of the Aegean Sea where he sacked the city of Smyma and then turned his attention to his next conquest, which would be the Ming dynasty in China. The preparations took up the next three years and as he was leading his army eastward he died, at age sixty-nine. He was buried in a magnificent tomb in Samarkand, and his surviving children were not strong enough to hold the empire together. For eleven years after the battle of Angora, the sons of the Muslim Baezid, who somehow managed to escape the disastrous battle, waged a civil war that nearly tore what was left of the empire to pieces. Finally, in 1413, Mehmed I crowned himself sultan and put the empire back together which allowed the Ottoman Empire to endure until its collapse at the end of the first world war in 1920.

Meanwhile, in China, the establishment of the Ming dynasty in 1368 marks the return of native rule over all of China for the first time in centuries. Between 1403 and 1424, the reign of Yongle was marked by five massive expeditions against the Mongols to the north, as well as campaigns in Vietnam. It was also a period of artistic excellence noted for elegant porcelains and textiles and for the production of numerous Buddhist icons for use at the court and as gifts to Tibet.

Between 1405 and 1433 Muslim, Grand Eunuch Zheng He (1371–1435) lead seven grand naval expeditions, some totaling three hundred ships and twenty-seven thousand sailors, reaching India and Persia as well as Africa. His concerns were primarily diplomatic, seeking to establish ties with other nations. Exotic animals such as giraffes, rhinoceroses, and lions were brought back to China for the amusement of the court.

In 1474, Mongol incursions into northern China helped spur the addition or extensions to the "Great Wall" This work continued until the end of the Ming dynasty around 1644.

During the Hundred Year's War, a seventeen-year-old French peasant. Joan of Arc led a French force in relieving the city of Orleans which had been under siege, by the English, since October 1428. According to the story, the young lady, at age sixteen, hear "voices" of Christian saints telling her to aid Charles in gaining the French throne and expelling the English from France. Convinced of the validity of her divine mission, Charles furnished Joan with a small force of troops which she led to Orleans. On April 29, as a French sortie distracted the English troops on the west side of the city, Joan entered unopposed by its eastern gate bringing needed supplies. She so inspired the French resistance, and over the next few weeks, she led charges and engaged in battles that eventually broke the siege and the English retreated. In the final month of the campaign, Joan led French forces to stunning victories at Reims, and later, when Charles VII was crowned King of France, Joan of Arc was there, kneeling at his feet.

In May 1430, while leading a military expedition against the English, she was captured by Bourguignon soldiers and sold to the English, who tried her for heresy. She was convicted of being a heretic and witch and on May 30. 1431, burned at the stake at Rouen. In 1920, Joan of Arc, already one of the great heroes of French history, was recognized as a Christian saint by the Roman Catholic Church.

On the other side of the world the Incas (1438–1533) incorporated a large portion of western South America, centered on the Andean Mountains, using conquest and peaceful assimilation. The Inca Empire also known as the Incan Empire and the Inka Empire was the largest empire in pre Columbian America and possibly the largest empire in the world in the early sixteenth century. The center of the empire was located in Cusco in modern-day Peru. The Inca civilization had originated in the highlands of Peru in the early thirteenth century and was conquered by the Spanish in 1572.

The Inca Empire was unique in that it lacked many features associated with civilization in the old world. In the word of one scholar, "The Incas lacked the use of wheeled vehicles. They lacked animals to ride and draft animals and they lacked the knowledge of iron and steel. Above all they lacked a system of writing, but despite these handicaps the Incas were still able to construct one of the greatest imperial states in human history."

In 1439, Johannes Gutenberg (Johannes Gensfleisch zur Laden zum Gutenberg), a German blacksmith and goldsmith, introduced printing to Europe. His invention of movable type led to the printing revolution and is widely regarded as the most important invention of the second millennium, the seminal event which ushered in the modern period of human history. It played a key role in the development of the Renaissance Reformation, the Age of Enlightenment, and the scientific revolution and laid the material basis for the modern knowledge-based economy and the spread of learning to the masses.

The Portuguese Empire (or Portuguese Overseas) was one of the largest and longest-lived empires in world history and the very first Colonial Empire. It existed for almost six centuries from the capture of Ceuta in 1415 (a strategically located North African Muslim enclave on the Mediterranean Sea) to the grant of sovereignty, to East Timor, in 2002.

The explorers feared what lay beyond Cape Bojador, and some thought that if you sailed below the cape it might not be possible to sail back. Once Gil Eanes, one of Henry's (Prince Henry the Navigator) captains, breached that psychological barrier, it became easier to further probe the west coast of Africa. During this period, the caravel was a major advancement that accelerated fifteenth century exploration. It was a ship that could be sailed closer to the wind than any other previous vessel and using this new technological advancement the Portuguese navigators were able to reach even more southerly latitudes, advancing down the coast about one degree per year. Senegal and Cape Verde Peninsula (present-day Dakar on Africa's west coast where the continent bulges out the farthest into the Atlantic Ocean) was reached in 1445. It was not until 1488, however, that Bartolomeu Dias rounded the Cape of Good Hope on the southern tip of Africa, proving false the view that had existed since Ptolemy that the Indian Ocean was landlocked.

In 1492, Christopher Columbus's discovery for Spain of the New World, which he believed to be Asia, led to disputes between the Spanish and Portuguese. These were eventually settled by the Treaty of Tordesillas in 1494 which divided the world outside of Europe between the Portuguese and the Spanish along a north–south meridian three hundred and seventy leagues or nine hundred and seventy miles west of the Cape Verde islands. However, as it was not possible at the time to correctly measure longitude the exact boundary was disputed by the two countries until 1777.

In 1497, Vasco da Gama left Portugal and rounded the Cape of Good Hope and continued along the East coast of Africa, crossed the Indian Ocean and reached Calcuta in southwestern India in May of 1498. In 1500 Pedro Alvares Cabral was dispatched for a second voyage to India; however, he was blown off course and made landfall on the Brazilian coast, which may have been an accidental discovery, but speculation has it that the Portuguese secretly knew of Brazil's existence in that it lay on their side of the Tordesillas line. Upon his return, Cabral recommended to the Portuguese King that Brazil be settled, and two follow-up voyages were sent in 1501 and 1503. The land was found to be abundant in pau-brasil, or brazilwood, from which it later inherited its name, but the failure to find gold or silver meant that for the time being Portuguese efforts would be concentrated on India.

As Portugal and Spain discovered the African continent, they also discovered that the slavery business could reap high rewards, and from 1400 through colonial times, it was a thriving business. The first report of bringing black slaves from Africa to Europe was in 1441, when a Portuguese captain named Anato capture twelve Africans in Cabo Branco (modern Mauritania) and took them to Portugal as slaves. In 1444, a group of over two hundred and thirty-five Africans were captured in the town of Lagos and brought back to Portugal. In 1452, the Portuguese started sugar plantations on the island of Madeira and used slaves to work the land. Even Christopher Columbus got into the slave business by bringing back several hundred slaves, the first transatlantic such shipment, from his second voyage to the Americas. He transported several hundred Taino people from the island of Hispaniola (modern Dominican Republic) back to Spain. To the Spanish credit, there was a minor uproar in Spain as to the legality of buying and selling slaves; however, it was short lived, and the slave trade became a part of European life.

In 1517, Martin Luther, a German professor of theology, composer, priest, and monk, rejected several teachings and practices of the Roman Catholic Church. He strongly disputed his understanding of the Catholic view on indulgences that freedom from God's punishment for sin could be purchased with money. His *Ninety-five Theses of 1517* set forth his views, and when he would not renounce all of his writings, as demanded by Pope Leo X, he was excommunicated and condemned as an outlaw by the emperor. Basically, Luther taught that salvation and, subsequently, eternal life are not earned by good deeds but are received only as the free gift of God's grace through the believer's faith in Jesus Christ as redeemer for sin. Those who identified with Martin were called Lutherans; however, Luther insisted on Christian or evangelical as the only acceptable names for individuals who professed Christ.

Luther's translation of the Bible into the vernacular (instead of Latin) made it more accessible to the masses, an event that had a tremendous impact on both the church and German culture. It fostered the development of a standard version of the German language, added several principles to the art of translation, and influenced the writing of an English translation, the Tyndale Bible. In two of his late works, Luther expressed antagonistic views toward Jews, writing that Jewish homes and synagogues should be destroyed, their money confiscated, and liberty curtailed. Condemned by virtually every Christian denomination, these statements and their influence on anti-Semitism have contributed to his controversial status, down through the ages.

The Spanish Armada (Grande y Felicisima Armada) was a fleet of one hundred and thirty ships that sailed from Corunaa, Spain, in August of 1588. The purpose was to escort an army from Flanders that was to invade England and overthrow Elizabeth I, which the Spanish hoped would put a stop to the harm being caused in the Spanish Netherlands by English and Dutch privateering. The battle hinged on poor decisions by the Duke of Medina Sidonia while he waited for word from the army and the timely attack by English ships that managed to scatter the Spanish fleet. In the ensuing Battle of Gravelines, the Spanish fleet was damaged and forced to abandon its rendezvous with the army who was blockaded in harbor by Dutch boats. The English lost several hundred men in the battle and eight ships out of the one hundred and ninety-seven, they and their Dutch allies put up as defense but over eight thousand Englishmen died of disease during the campaign which attests to the deplorable conditions that festered on the sailing ships of the day. The Spanish lost at least thirty-five ships and over twenty thousand men during the brief campaign.

The following year, the English organized a similar campaign against Spain, the Drake–Norris Expedition, which was unsuccessful, had serious economic consequences, and saw the loss of thousands of English lives and many ships. Queen Elizabeth went to Tilbury to encourage her forces and the next day gave to them what was considered her most-famous speech.

"My loving people, we have been persuaded by some that are acreful of our safety, to take heed how we commit ourselves to armed multitudes for fear of treachery; but, I do assure you, I do not desire to live to distrust my faithful and loving people. Let tyrants fear, I have always so behaved myself, that under God I have placed my chiefest strength and safe guard in the loyal hearts and goodwill of my subjects; and, therefore, I come amongst you as you see at this time, not for my recreation and disport, but being resolved, in the midst and heat of battle, to live or die amongst you all - to lay down my God, and for my kingdoms, and for my people, my honour and my blood even in the dust..."

It ended after much "I," "My" sharing with, "by your obedience to my general, by your concord in the camp, and your valour in the field, we shall shortly have a famous victory over those enemies of MY God, of MY kingdoms, and for MY people, MY honour and MY blood eve in the dust."

After the victory, typhus swept the fleet, killing off thousands of the English mariners who had won the battle. Elizabeth failed in her promise to pay the sailors, and of the few who did survive, even of the crew of the royal warship, Elizabeth, most expired destitute in the gutters of Margate. (Margate is a seaside town in the district of Thanet in Kent, England, about thirty-eight miles east-north-east of Maidstone.)

In Elizabeth I's world, William Shakespeare was the man of the hour. He was born in 1564 in Stratford-upon-Avon, and he also died there in 1616. Little is known about Shakespeare's activities between 1585 and 1592. He may have taught school but it seems more probable that shortly after he finished school (King Edward VI Grammar School in Stratford) in 1585, he went to London to begin his apprenticeship as an actor. Due to the plague, the London theaters were closed between June 1592 and April 1594. During that period, Shakespeare probably had some income from his Patron, Henry Wriothesley, Earl of Southdmpton, to whom he dedicated his first two poems. In 1594, he joined the Lord Chamberlain's company of actors, the most popular of the companies acting at Court. In 1599, a group of his peers formed a syndicate to build and operate a new playhouse: The Globe, which became the most-famous theater of its time.

Between 1593 and 1601, he wrote sonnets 1–126 addressed to a beloved friend, a handsome and noble young man, and sonnets 127–152 to a malignant but fascinating "Dark Lady."

In his poems and plays, Shakespeare invented thousands of words, often combining or contorting Latin, French, and native roots. His impressive expansion of the English language, according to the Oxford English Dictionary, includes such words as arch-villain, birthplace, bloodsucking, courtship, dewdrop, downstairs, fanged, heartsore, hunchbacked, leapfrog, misquote, pageantry, radiance, schoolboy, stillborn, watchdog and zany.

Shakespeare wrote more than thirty plays which are usually divided into four categories: histories, comedies, tragedies and romances. During his lifetime he publish just eighteen of the works, the balance did not appear until the publication of the First Folio in 1623, five years after his death. Nonetheless, his contemporaries recognized Shakespeare for this plays and poems and the Chamberlain's Men rose to become the leading dramatic company in London, installed as members of the Royal house hold in 1603.

During the two hundred years between 1400 and 1600, war was a constant, and it started with the English invasion of Scotland (1400), Mongols War with Syria (1400), Battle of Angora (1402),

Glyndwr Rising (1400–1420), Battle of Ankara (140w), Ottoman Interregnum (1402–1413), Conquest of the Canary Islands (1402–1496), Percy Rebellion (1403), Scrope Rebellion (1405), Armagnac–Burgundian Civil War (1407–1435), Polish–Lithuanian Teutonic War (1409–1411), Ming–Kotte War (1410), Cabochien Revolt (1413), Hunger War (1414), Oldcastle Revolt (1414), Battle of Agincourt (1415) (part of the Hundred Years' War) took place in County of Saint-Poe near Caiais, France.

Henry V crossed the English Channel with eleven thousand men in August and laid siege to Harfleur in Normandy. After five weeks, the town surrendered, but Henry lost half his men to disease and battle casualties. He decided to march northeast to Calais where he would meet the English fleet for his return to England; however, at Agincourt, on October 25, 1415, a vast French army of twenty thousand men stood in his path. The battlefield was less than a thousand yards of open ground between two woods which prevented largescale maneuvers, and this worked to Henry's advantage. The English stood their ground as the French knights, weighed down by their heavy armor, began a slow advance across the muddy battlefield.

The English met the advance with a heavy bombardment of English archers, who wielded innovative longbows with a range of two hundred and fifty yards. French cavalrymen tried and failed to overwhelm the English positions but were no match for the English archers who held their ground behind a line of pointed stakes. As more and more French knights made their way onto the battlefield, their mobility decreased further. Henry sent in lightly equipped men with swords and axes, and the unencumbered English massacred the French. The French lost six thousand men while Henry lost only several hundred. Despite the odds against him, Henry had won one of the great victories in military history. This English victory was the first earth war viewed by inhabitants of another planet.

The other wars include the following: Lam Son uprising (1418), Oei Invasion (1419), Hussite Wars (1419–1435), Bavarian War (1420–1422), War of the Oxen (1421–1422), Siege of Constantinople (1422), Gollub War (1422), War of L'Aquila (1423–1424), Wars in Lombardy (1425–1454), Dano–Hanseatic

War (1426–1435), Shocho uprising (1428), Neville–Neville Feud (1428–1443), Polish–Teutonic War (1431–1435), First Irmandiño (1431–1435), Lithuanian Civil War (1431–1435), Albanian Revolt (1432–1436), Engelbrekt rebellion (1434–1436), Luchuan–Pingmian campaigns (1436–1449), Praguerie (1440), Old Zurich War (1440–1446), Battle of Torvioll (1444), Soest Feud (1444), Saxon Fratricidal War (1446–1451), Flower War (Aztec) (1446–early 1500s), Tumu Crisis (1449–1449), First Margrave War (1449–1450), Revolt of Ghent (1449–1453), Kottle conquest of the Jaffna Kingdom (1449–1454), Jack Cade Rebellion (1450), Navarrese Civil War (1451–1455), Fall of Constantinople (1453), Percy–Neville feud (1453–1454), Thirteen Years' War (1454–1466), Mexica Flower war (1445–1519), Bonville–Courtenay feud (1455), Wars of the Roses (1455–1487), Siege of Belgrade (1456), Ayutthaya–Lan Na War (1456–1474), Bavarian War (1459–1463), Rebellion of Cao Qin (Ming) (1461), The Night Attack (1462), War of the Succession of Stelin (1464–1472), Moroccan revolt (1465), Ballaban's Campaign (1465), War of Public Weal (1465), Wars of Liege (1465–1468), First Irmandiño (1467–1469), Onin War (1467–1477), War of the Priests (1467–1479), Bohemian War (1468–1478), Dano–Swedish War (1470–1471), First Utrecht Civil War (1470–1474), Cham–Vietnamese War (1471), Burgundian Wars (1474–1477), War of the Castilian Succession (1475–1479), Ottoman–Moldavian War (1476), Austrian–Hungarian War (1477–1488), Siege of Rhodes (1480), Saltpeter War (1480–1510), Second Utrecht Civil War (1481–1483), War of Ferrara (1482–1484), Granada War (1482–1492), Buckingham's rebellion (1483), Flemish Revolt (1483–1485), Mieres Uprising (1484), Mad War (1485–1488), Stafford and Lovell Rebellion (1486–1487), Simmel Rebellion (1486–1487), Kaga Rebellion (1487–1488), Flemish Revolt (1487–1492), Yorkshire rebellion (1489), First Muscovite–Lithuanian War (1492–1494), Bundschuh movement (1493–1517), Italian War with France (1494–1498), Russo–Swedish War (1495–1497), Cornish Rebellion (1497), Second Cornish Uprising (1497), Warbeck Rebellion (1497), Swabian War (1499), Conquest of Melilla (1499), Rebellion of Alpujarras (1499–1501), Ottoman–

Venetian War (1499–1503), Italian War with France (1499–1504), Second Muscovite–Lithuanian War (1500–1503), Dano–Swedish War (1501–1512), Persian–Uzbek Wars (1502–1510), Guelders Wars (1502–1543), Landshut War of Succession (1503–1505), Portuguese–Mamluk naval war (1505–1517), Third Muscovite–Lithuanian War (1507–1508), War of the League of Cambrai (1508–1516), Battle of Diu (Portuguese battles in the Indian Ocean) (1509), Ottoman Civil War (1509–1512), Prince of Anhua Rebellion (1510), Hvar Rebellion (1510–1514), Portuguese conquest of Goa (1510), Friulian Revolt (1511), Sahkulu Rebellion (1511), Spanish–Taino War (1511–1529), Malayan–Portuguese War (1511–1641), Bengali conquest of Chittagong (1512–1516), Fourth Muscovite–Lithuanian War (1512–1522), Poor Conrad Rebellion (1514), Gyorgy Dozsa Rebellion (1514), Battle of Chaldiran (1514), Slovene Peasant Revolt (1515–1523), Arumer Zwarte Hoop (1515–1523), Ottoman–Mamluk War (1516–1517), Tran Cao Rebellion (1516–1521), Prince of Ning rebellion (1519–1521), Polish–Teutonic War (1519–1521), Spanish conquest of the Aztec Empire (1519–1521), Revolt of the Brotherhoods (1519–1522), Hildesheim Diocesan Feud (1519–1523), Jelali revolts (1519–1659), Revolt of the Comuneros (1520–1521), First Battle of Tamao (Ming) (1521), Swedish War of Liberation (1521–1523), Italian War (1521–1526), Musso War (1521–1532), Knight's Revolt (1522), Second Battle of Tamao (1522), Siege of Rhodes (1522), Franconian War (1523), German Peasants' War (1524–1525), Dalecarlian Rebellion (1524–1533), Amicable Grant Revolt (1525), War of the League of Cognac (1526–1543), Battle of Mohacs (1526), Sinhalese–Portuguese War (1527–1638), Spanish Conquest of Yucatan (1527–1697), Hungarian Campaign (1527–1528), Ethiopian–Adal War (1529–1543), First War of Kappel (1529), Balkan Campaign (1529), Siege of Vienna (1529), Inca Civil War (1529–1532), Little War in Hungary (1530–1552), Second War of Kappel (1531), Spanish Conquest of the Inca Empire (1532–1572), Ottoman–Safavid War (1532–1555), Yaqui Wars (1533–1929) (Part of the Mexican–Indian Wars and American–Indian Wars—four hundred years), Silken Thomas Rebellion (1534), Munster Rebellion (1534–1535), Count's Feud (1534–1536), Fifth

Muscovite–Lithuanian War (1534–1541), Taungoo–Hanthawaddy War (1534–1541), Iguape War Brazil (1534–1546), Schmalkaldic War (1536–1537), Pilgrimage of Grace (1536–1537), Italian War (1536–1538), Bigod's Rebellion (1537), Conquistador Civil War in Peru (1537–1548), Taungoo–Ava War (1538–1545), Ottoman–Portuguese conflicts (1538–1557), Peasant's Rebellion in Telemark (1540), Mixton War (1540–1542), Dacke War (1542–1543), Italian War (1542–1546), Koch–Ahom conflicts (1543–1568), Taungoo–Mrauk-U War (1545–1547), Schmalkaldic War (1546–1547), Burmese–Siamese War (1547–1549), Jiajing wokou raids (1547–1565), Revolt of the Pitauds (France) (1548–1549), Prayer Book Rebellion (1549), Buckinghamshire Oxfordshire Rising (1549), Kett's Rebellion (1549), Chichimeca War (1550–1590), Italian War (1551–1559), Second Margrave War (1552–1556), Siege of Kazan (1552), Kazan Rebellion (1552–1556), Wyatt's Rebellion (1554), Russo–Swedish War (1554–1557), Saukrieg (1555–1558), France Antarctique (1555–1567), Ottoman Conquest of Habesh (1557–1578), Ottoman–Portuguese conflicts (1558–1566), Shane O'Neill's Rebellion (1558–1567), Livonian War (1558–1583), Portuguese invasion of Jaffna Kingdom (1560), French Wars of Religion (1562–1598), Burmese–Siamese War (1563–1564), Northern Seven Years' War (1563–1570), Philippine Revolts against Spain (1567–1872) (three hundred and five years), Burmese–Siamese War (1568–1570), Morisco Revolt (1568–1571), Marian Civil War (1568–1573), Eighty Years' War (1568–1648), First Desmond Rebellion (1569–1573), Rising of the North (1569–1570), War of the League of the Indies (1570–1574), Ottoman–Venetian War (1570–1573), Ishiyama Hongan-ji War (1570–1580), Russo–Crimean War (1571), Mughal Invasion of Bengal (1572–1576), Croatian–Slovene Peasant Revolt (1573), Danzig rebellion (1575–1577), Castilian War (1578), Ottoman–Safavid War (1578–1590), Tensho Iga War (1579–1581), Second Desmond Rebellion (1579–1583), War of the Portuguese Succession (1580–1583), Ottoman–Portuguese conflicts (–15891580), Cologne War (1583–1588), Burmese–Siamese War (1584–1593), Anglo–Spanish War (1585–1604), War of the Polish Succession (1587–1588), Beylerbeyi Event (1589), Russo–Swedish

War (1590–1595), Portuguese Invasion of Jaffna Kingdom (1591–1593), Kosinski Uprising (1591–1593), Rappenkrieg War (Swiss peasants) (1591–1594), Ayutthayan–Cambodian War (1591–1594), Long War (1591–1606), Japanese invasions of Korea (1592–1598), Strasbourg Bishops' War (1592–1604), Cambodian–Spanish War (1593–1597), Moldavian Magnate Wars (1593–1617), Nalyvaiko Uprising (1593–1596), Burmese–Siamese War (1594–1605), Nine Years' War Ireland (1594–1603), Himara Revolt (1596), Oxfordshire Rising (1596), Cudgel War (Finnish peasants) (1596–1597), and the Sigismund War. (1598–1599).

Wars recorded: 246

16

Teren: 1400 to 1599

The spaceship Exodus IV lifted off from the world space center in Baghdad, promptly at 5:00, as planned and arched past the moon minutes later on its way to Teren-Gamma, at the far edge of the Milky Way. The booster rocket was the solid propeller type that provided the raw power to lift the giant out of Teren's gravity field and get it into space where the nuclear-powered spaceship could accelerate to a speed three times the speed of light. The trip would take over six months, but the passengers, all in the small-man format, were already in a state of suspended animation that would last for the duration of the trip. The flight crews, of which there were six, would rotate in and out of the suspended animation which they called "deep sleep" over the course of the next six months. There were always three crews available, in the awake mode, to insure a safe and uneventful trip.

After the booster rocket burned, it automatically unlatched and floated back to Teren to be reused. The nuclear-powered spaceship immediately went to full power mode, and the acceleration was so great that each passenger had to be in a special air-foam-controlled seat that served to keep ribs and organs from being broken and smashed. Once at top speed, the shield deflectors automatically engaged which was a powerful electromagnetic field that would deflect space debris out of the spacecraft's path. Without the protective shield, the spacecraft could only fly at about Mach I as there was just too many floating rocks and chunks of past stars and planets that littered the route. One of the astronauts equated the space shield to the cowcatcher that was standard on all the trains that traversed Western America when the buffalo still roamed.

The two-hundred-foot long spacecraft looked like an inverted ice-cream cone with the pilot compartment at the very tip of the cone's tapered nose. On board were almost forty thousand men, women, and children, and all the personal belongings they would need to start a new life. There were already one hundred and seventy-five million people on Teren-Gamma, half of which had been born there. This added contingent would bring much-needed skills, of every kind, to the new planet that had first been colonized just fifteen years earlier. On Teren-Gamma, several new towns were being built on continents that had not yet been inhabited, and the pioneer experiences, of the West Americans, were about to be repeated. There were no hostile Indians, but the wildlife was a challenge in that there were dinosaur-type creatures that seemed to enjoy munching on the human body. Fortunately, most of the critters had been zapped and reduced to ninety-five percent of their original size, but even the miniature versions were aggressive and could inflict a nasty bite. The construction workers had to employ a laser barrier around the jobsites to keep the little devils out, and the authorities were considering exterminating the remaining pests, but the animal rights activist were protesting that solution.

Teren-Gamma had three moons, each about half the size of the earth and Teren moons, and they were grouped relatively close together, which meant that full moon nights were almost as light as twilight. The moons were not pocked with craters and mountains but were smooth and shiny, almost like giant agate marbles. The scientists projected the theory that at one time, the moons had passed very close to a sun and that the surface had actually melted, like flowing lava. Somehow they had escaped the suns gravitational pull and came to their current location millions of years ago. As on Teren-Beta, the moons exerted a dramatic tidal action on the planet's oceans, and as a result, the beaches that may have been there in centuries past had been eroded down to bare bedrock, and in just fifteen years, the scientists had noticed that the land masses were in fact shrinking. Since each of the nineteen continents were so large, no one was worried about being washed away, but of course there were few seaside communities.

Back on mother Teren, the population had been reduced by the Exodus flights but still stood at 2.2 billion, almost four times the earth's population. Everyone agreed that the five colonized planets could continue to accept immigration, and for now, further space transfers would be on a need-only basis. The pressure was off, and the CEO in Jerusalem was pleased with the progress that his people were making as was his creator.

The planets so far colonized were Teren-Alpha (eight hundred million), TerenBeta (five hundred and eighty-five million), Teren-Gamma (one hundred and seventy-five million), Teren-Delta (one hundred and forty million), and Teren-Epsilon (twenty-six million).

Technology wise, by the year 1600, Teren and all its satellite planets had exceeded what man would be doing on earth in the year 2500. The brain trust on earth was just not there; too many brilliant and creative brains had been left on the bloody battlefields of the planet, and both God and the earth's Jesus were deeply saddened by the earthlings' inability to solve their petty squabbles. The contrast between earth and Teren was mind altering, and it was now proven, beyond a shadow of a doubt, that there was an alternative to the never-ending carnage that went on all over the blue planet, which from space appeared to be a beautiful, serene, tranquil, harmonious, and pleasant place to rest.

At least that is what it looked like from space as a small spaceship from the planet Teren made its first fly-by in the earth's sky on October 25, 1415.

The space probe Teren-Alpha 9 flown by twenty-five humans, in the small-man format, had never ventured this far from their home planet. They were in an unknown galaxy exploring a small solar system, and they had been excited for days as a small blue planet was materializing out of the darkness that had a striking resemblance to their ancestral home of Teren. As they closed in on the beautiful floating marble, they noticed that it had a single moon, just like Teren, and as they came closer and could start seeing surface features, they were dumfounded by the similarity to mother Teren. The oceans, the land masses, and the poles were almost carbon copies of Teren, and as they zoomed in closer and established a planet orbit, at one-hundred-mile level, they, with the naked eye, could see the mountain ranges, great deserts, vast oceans, as well as the polar caps. It was uncanny. It was like they were orbiting Teren. The same clouds circling the globe and the land-to-water ratios are all strikingly similar, and once they engaged their telescopes, they could see lifeforms that looked identical to what they saw when they looked in the mirror. The commander immediately send detailed communications about their location and the nature of their discovery and asked for instructions. Should they just observe and gain as much information as possible? Should they make close fly-bys? Should they land and make their presence known to the indigenous population? These were all the questions he framed in his report.

The crew of Teren-Alpha 9 was glued to their telescopes, and as they scanned the lands below them, they watched in horror as two great armies collided near the French town of Agincourt. Thousands of armed men descended on one another, and when the carnage ceased, the battlefield was covered with almost seven thousand dead and dying humans. The spacemen were shocked; they had never even envisioned such behavior other than reading ancient history about what went on in Teren before the coming of their beloved Christ.

As Jesus and God looked down on the agonizing scene taking place in the midst of the blazing fall colors that this region of France was sporting, they noticed that the beauty of God's land was somehow overshadowing the anguish cries of the dying and wounded who littered the battlefield. After one thousand and four hundred years of watching man's inhumanity to man, the creator and his son certainly were not shocked, but they were concerned and wondered how the Terenlings were going to react to the horrors being played out below them by a race of beings that were in fact their brothers.

"Son, please inform your brother that the Terenians have discovered earth and suggest that they be given instructions to return to Teren Alpha without making contact with the human inhabitants."

"Yes, my father."

17

Earth: 1600 to 1799

A golden age is a period in a field of endeavor when great tasks were accomplished, and there have been many since man started recording the planet's history. There was the Golden Age of Ancient Egypt, of Athens, of Latin Literature, of East Indian culture, and of Christians in Ireland. There was the Islamic Golden Ages (622–1258), the Spanish and Portuguese Golden Ages, and hundreds of minor events that regional peoples celebrate and remember as their particular golden age.

The period between 1600 and 1800, while carrying no specific or monumental golden age, was for the Japanese a period of relative peace and stability, following centuries of warfare and disruption. The Edo or Tokugawa period lead to expansion of the national economy and the increase in agricultural production, transportation infrastructure, commerce, population, and literacy. Although the imperial court continues to exist and maintains nominal authority, the Tokugawa shogunate, based in Edo, wields the actual political power. Control of the country was divided between the shogunate and approximately two hundred and seventy regional military lords (daimyo) who owe their direct power to the shogun while ruling their own domains. The central government stays strong and enforces strict social policies over domestic issues while keeping a firm limitation on all foreign trade and exchange.

The merchant and artisan classes reap the benefits from the Edo period's prosperity and urban expansion. Cities like Osaka and Kyoto thrive while new castle towns are built by the daimyo and samurai masters. Using the wealth, city residents temporarily escape official restrictions by enthusiastically patronizing the pleasure quarters being established in all large cities and the courtesans, entertainers, prostitutes, teahouses, theaters, and restaurants found there. New forms of highly entertaining drama, literature, painting, and printmaking cater to popular trends of the day, making the Edo period an active and innovative time for the arts.

In China, the Ming dynasty is weakening, and this paves the way for the Manchu takeover. As they come to power, calling themselves the Qing dynasty, they control large portions of Central Asia and most of the other neighboring regions. China becomes one of the wealthier nations in the world due to efficient production and trade in tea and other luxury goods, such as, silk and porcelain. This export of Chinese goods has a profound effect on the visual arts of much of Europe, influencing architecture, textiles, and ceramics and creating a taste for new materials, such as, lacquer goods. The new Manchus masters (now called the Qing dynasty) decrees that all Chinese men shave their foreheads and wear their hair in a long queue or plait, just another way to control the conquered peoples. Between 1662 and 1722, the emperor is Kangxi, and he commissions much historical writing, as well as dictionaries and other reference tools, and reestablishes imperial workshops for the production of porcelain, lacquer metalwork, and other goods.

The island of Taiwan is added to the Qing empire, and the pirate Zheng Chengqong, known in the Western world as Koxinga, who had been Taiwan's absolute ruler, is sent into exile. (Koxinga had become a legion by defeating both the Portuguese and Dutch traders in 1650 sea battles.)

The Jesuit priest Pere d'Entrecolle provides detailed descriptions of the organization of the porcelain factories and the techniques used in the making of ceramics and thus gives the European makers a leg up on producing porcelain and ceramics to Chinese standards.

In 1717, the Qing dynasty halts the invasion of Tibet by the Mongol Zunghar, and by 1720, they gain control, installing a new Dalai Lama loyal to the Qing court.

In the Americas, South of the Rio Grande, the modern world is overtaking the local peoples and not for the good. Those identified as criollo, people of European descent born in the Americas, are on the rise, and the indigenous population continues it calamitous decline.

Period writers compose revealing chronicles about the disappearing Inca culture, and Potosi, the silver-rich city which is the source of the Peruvian wealth, is the fifth most populous city on the face of the planet by 1620. The heartland of Peru is marked by the political and cultural divisions between the Pacific coast city of Lima, where fifty percent of the population is criollo, and the city of Cuzco, the high Andean seat of Inca civilization, where the population is predominantly native. Missionary activities in the high areas lead to extensive conversions of the Cuzco natives. Cults, such as, the Virgin of Guapulo, the Virgin of Copacabana, the Virgin of Cocharcas, and the Virgin of Belen, are extremely popular with the mountain people.

According to Incan lore, after a great flood, the god Viracocha arose from Lake Titicaca to create the world. He commanded the sun and moon and stars to rise and then created the first humans out of rock and commanded them to go forth and populate the world. Lake Titicaca is the birthplace of the Incas, whose spirits return to their origin, in the lake, upon death. (In 2000, a submerged temple, six hundred and sixty feet long was discovered on the lake's bottom. It is believed to be nearly 1500 years old.)

While Spain is trying to manage their South American charges, all kinds of competitors are nipping at their heels. The Dutch, the English, the Portuguese as well as the persistent pirates and privateers are all trying to muscle in on the silver trade, and Spain tries to address these concerns by banning Manila Galleons from sailing to Lima and by attempting to stop transshipment of Asian goods; however, the interlopers are too numerous to police and Spain loses ships and treasure at an alarming rate.

In 1607, Captain John Smith, with a charter from King James I, settled in North America at the mouth of the James River, and the colonists faced real challenges in finding a stable source of food and support. Conflicts with the local natives added to their challenges, but experiments with growing tobacco proved successful, and exporting the product to Europe contributed to a comfortable lifestyle for many of Virginia's gentry over the next century. Many of the settlers were indentured servants who signed four- or seven-year contracts in turn for their passage across the Atlantic Ocean. Once free of their contracts, the colony gave them small tracts of land; the exception to this rule was the black African slaves.

Lord Baltimore founded the colony of Maryland, and his charter allowed for the establishment of churches of all religions. By the last third of the century, the two colonies had established strong economic, and social ties and expansive farmlands along the rivers, manned by a never-ending supply of African slaves, created an aristocratic way of life for the wealthy class. The other immigrants, mostly German, Scots, and Irish populated the Shenandoah Valley and the Appalachian Mountains, and on these frontiers they built small cabins and cultivated corn and wheat.

In the area around present-day New York City, Henry Hudson led the establishment of a colony he named New Netherlands, and its capital, New Amsterdam, looked like a Dutch town with canals, brick houses, gabled roofs, and winding streets. In 1664, the British took control of the area and changed the name to New York. The Dutch settlers were allowed to retain their properties and worship as they pleased, and the Colonial Dutch style of life remained pervasive in the area throughout the eighteenth century.

In 1611, William Penn received a charter from Charles II for a large tract of land west of the Delaware River and Penn encouraged religious dissenters like the Quakers, Amish, Baptists, and Mennonites to settle his lands. The area grew rapidly with many of the settlers coming from the Rhine region in German as well as large numbers of Scots and Irish who settled the rural areas of Pennsylvania. In 1685, the area's population was nine thousand, and within a hundred years, Philadelphia had over thirty thousand inhabitants.

In 1675, King Phillip's War erupts in New England between colonists and Native Americans. The bloody war rages up and down the Connecticut River valley, in Massachusetts, and in Rhode Island colonies. In the end, six hundred colonists are killed and three thousand Native Americans die, including women and children on both sides. The chief of the Wampanoags is finally hunted down and killed, ending the war and ending the independent power of the Native Americans in the greater New England areas.

Across the continent, it was not until 1579 that the west coast of North America was visited by an English explorer, Sir Francis Drake, who landed north of today's San Francisco and claimed the area for England, calling it New Albion. Later, in the eighteenth century, British claims to portions of the west coast of North America were based on the Drake's visit. One of the most important consequences of these claims is that charters for the British colonies, on the Atlantic coast, went from sea to sea, and this was the foundation of the US claim to its current territory.

In Southwestern America, the Yaqui Indians were the main participants in a war with Spanish, Mexican, and Americans that lasted from 1533 to 1929. For three hundred and ninety-six years, the Yaqui endured the overrunning of their lands by first the Spanish who were looking for slaves and later by the Mexicans in their quest for the "silver rock." At one battle, with the Spanish, they put seven thousand men in the field, and while the Spanish were soundly beaten, the Yaquis lost thousands. Between 1608 and 1610, the Spanish repeatedly attacked the Yaqui people, and in desperation, they requested that the Jesuits come into their villages to do missionary work and help with economic development, thinking that this would help bring peace. It did not. In 1740, the Yaqui allied with the neighboring Mayo tribe to force the Spanish off their lands, but the battles went on for another one hundred and ninety years. After the Mexicans gained their independence from Spain, they picked up where the Spanish had left off and continued killing Yaquis.

In 1916, Mexico's governor Adolpho de la Huerta made an attempt to stop the bloodshed, but the next president changed the policy, and the Yaqui–Mexican wars continued. Their last battle was with the US Cavalry in January of 1918. It broke the back of the resistance, and in 1939, Mexican President Cardenas granted the Yaqui tribe official recognition and title to their land.

Down under, in Australia, most historians attribute the discovery to English explorer James Cook, but Macassan traders sailing from modern-day Indonesia were possibly the first to discover the vast continent. In 1606, a Dutch vessel, Duyfken, made landfall on the North coast, in the Gulf of Carpentaria, near Cape York Peninsula. The Dutch named the new discovery Arnhem Land and thus became the earliest known Europeans to reach Australia. It was not until 1770 when Cook first made landfall and claimed the expansive "no-man's land" for the British crown. Following Cook's initial exploration, the British established their first permanent settlement, a penal colony, in New South Wales in 1786 at Botany Bay, present-day Sydney. In 1799, the Black War begins, a six-year battle waged by Aborigines against white settlements in the Hawkesbury and Parramatta areas of New South Wales. On Tasmania, the island off the south coast, it is reported that the settlers walked shoulder to shoulder the length and breadth of the island and killed every Aborigine they found, thus solving their long-time feud with native peoples.

In Europe, continuous warfare and political instability dominate the seventeenth and eighteenth centuries; however, when the wealthy noblemen are not competing for power, they seem happy to support the arts. Scores of artists are employed in the various European capitals; however, in other burgeoning cities, such as, Dresden. Munich, Berlin, Warsaw, Prague, and Bratislava, the demand for their talent is extremely high. The rift between Catholics and Protestants continues to cause conflict and dynastic struggles among ambitious princes ensure continual violence. The Baroque style is the in thing, and throughout the German-speaking countries, literature and music flourish along with architecture, painting, and industry, with heavy Chinese influences.

In 1618, a predominantly Protestant city, a mob of citizens angrily throw the Habsburg governors from a castle window and thus begins the Thirty Years' War, in which the animosities fueled by the Reformation erupt in a generation-long conflict. The endless battles disrupt the training of art apprentices, and when peace finally comes, in 1648, few artists are available, and the commissions thus go to Italian and French artists.

In 1683, the Ottoman armies sweep westward through Hungary and lay siege to Vienna. The Polish King John III and Eugene of

Savoy at last relieves that city, and the Ottomans are driven back to their former borders, but the memory of the Ottoman campaign leaves a profound impression on the arts in the Habsburg Lands and in Vienna.

Throughout Europe, the rich and famous are on the leading edge of a construction bonanza. Prince Savoy builds two palaces near Vienna, Lower Belvedere, and Upper Belvedere. Charles IV begins Karlskirche Church which features two-feet standing columns adorned with elements that allude to the Pillars of Hercules, the Temple of Solomon, and the monuments to the Roman emperors Trojan and Marcus Aurelius. Near Kuks in Bohemia, Count Sporck founds the Bethlehem Forest Park—a magnificent integration of art and nature. The park is adorned with Biblical scenes carved out of natural outcrops of sandstone. In Munich, the interior of the Amalienburg Pavilion is reminiscent of a jewel box, painted in pastel colors and adorned with mirrors, porcelain, and crystal chandeliers. Near Staffelstein, Germany, the architect Neumann commences work on the Church of Vierzehnheiligen where ingenious intersecting ovals contain a central shrine and later Venetian painter Tiepolo creates ceiling frescoes in pastel colors that suit the brightness of the Neumann interior. At Potsdam, near Berlin, construction starts on the Palace of Sanssouci (Without a Care), a summer retread for Frederick II designed by Diterichs. The building was situated atop a terrace garden planted with fruit trees and adorned with a central staircase that linked the place to the extensive parks and waterworks. In the Bavarian town of Bayreuth, the Margrave's Opera House is completed and embellished with gilding and lit with hundreds of candles and is meant for an aristocratic audience and closed to those outside the court. In 1754, architect Zimmermann completed Die Wies, a delightful church in southern Germany. The walls are pierced with large windows, and the interior is encrusted with stucco ornament as delicate as molded sugar. The Frescoed ceiling is on the theme of the Last Judgment where Christ sits on a rainbow above figures in courtly poses. Die Wies becomes a popular destination for pilgrims and offers them a vision of paradise full of grace and light. In Fertod, Hungary, the Esterhazy family, one of the richest in the Habsburg Empire, build a summer palace that is painted yellow ochre and outfitted with French windows, sweeping enfilades, and formal gardens in the manner of Versifies. In 1798, Alois Senefelder of Munich invents the lithography, a printmaking technique that is widely used by the artists of the day, like Schinkel, Goya, and Menzel.

The arts flourish all across Europe. It became bigger and better and is coupled with the baroque and frescos to give the illusions that the wealthy and famous wish to heap upon themselves.

The art withstanding war is never far away, and in Japan, the Sekigahara Campaign started in 1600, and the Agrafa Revolt started that year as well. Other wars are as follows: Franco–Savoyard War (1600–1601), Navajo Wars (1600–1866), Polish–Swedish War (1600–1611), Dutch–Portuguese War (1602–1663), Ottoman–Safavid War (1603–1618), Polish–Muscovite War (1605–1618), Bolotnikov Rebellion (1606–1607), Zebrzydowski Rebellion (1606–1608), War of the Julich Succession (1609–1614), Invasion of Ryukyu (1609), First Anglo–Powhatan War (1610–1614), Ingrian War (1610–1617), Ioannina Revolt (1611), Kalmar War (1612–1613), Rappenkrieg (1612–1614), Equinoctial France War (1612–1615), Burmese–Siamese War (1613–1614), Siege of Osaka (1614–1615), Mataram Conquest of Surabaya (1614–1625), Uskok War (1615–1618), Ahom–Mughal conflicts (1615–1637), Tepehuan Revolt (1612–1620), Polish–Swedish War (1617–1618), Spanish Conquest of Peten (1618–1697), Maya (1618–1697), Bundner Wirren (1618–1639), Thirty Years' War (1618–1648), Qing conquest of the Ming (1618–1683), Ahom–Mughal conflicts (1619–1682), Polish–Ottoman War (1620–1621), Early Mughal–Sikh War (1621–1635), War of the Vicuñas and Basques (1622–1625), Second Anglo–Powhatan War (1622–1632), Ottoman–Safavid War (1623–1639), Zhmaylo Uprising (1625), Relief of Genoa (1625), Polish–Swedish War (1626–1629), Peasants' War in Upper Austria (1626–1636), First Manchu invasion of Korea (1627), Trinh–Nguyen War (1627–1672), War of the Mantuan Succession (1628–1631), Fedorovych Uprising (1630), Smolensk War (1632–1634), Polish–Ottoman War (1633–1634), Pequot War (1634–1638), Sulyma

Uprising (1635), Franco–Spanish War (1635–1659), Second Manchu invasion of Korea (1636–1637), Pavlyuk Uprising (1637), Shimabara Rebellion (1637–1638), Ostryanyn Uprising (1638), Revolt of the va-nu-pieds (France) (1639), First Bishops' War (1639), Second Bishops' War (1640), Catalan Revolt (1640–1659), Portuguese Restoration War (1640–1668), Beaver Wars (Iroquois/France) (1640–1701), Irish Confederate Wars (1641–1653), First War of Castro (1641–1644), First English Civil War (1642–1646), Cambodian–Dutch War (1643–1644), Torstenson War (1643–1645), Kieft's War (1643–1645), Third Anglo–Powhatan War (1644–1646), Scotland in the Wars of the Three Kingdoms (1644–1651), Cretan War (1645–1669), Moscow uprising (1648), Khmelnytsky Uprising (1648–1657), First Fronde (1648–1649), Second English Civil War (1648–1649), Third English Civil War (1649–1651), Mughal–Safavid War (1649–1653), Cromwellian Conquest of Ireland (1649–1653), Second War of Castro (1649), Second Fronde (1650–1653), Dusseldorf Cow War (1651), Kostka–Napierski Uprising (1651), Keian Uprising (1651), Three Hundred and Thirty Five Years' War (Isles of Scilly vs Rep. of the Netherlands (1651–1986), First Anglo–Dutch War (1652–1654), Russian–Manchu border conflicts (1652–1689), Swiss Peasant War (1653), Morning Star Rebellion (1653), First Swedish War on Bremen (1654), Russo–Polish War (1654–1667), Anglo–Spanish War (1654–1660), Peach Tree War (1655), Varazdin rebellion (1655–1656), Second Northern War (1655–1660), Cinar Incident (1656), Russo–Swedish War (1656–1658), Dano–Swedish War (1657–1658), Druze Power Struggle (1658–1667), Brunei Civil War (1660–1673), Siege of Fort Zeelandia (1661–1663), Copper Riot (1662), Burmese–Siamese War (1662–1665), Austro–Turkish War (1663–1664), Lubomirski's Rebellion (1665–1666), Second Anglo–Dutch War (1665–1667), Kongo Civil War (1665–1709), Second Swedish War on Bremen (1666), Polish–Cossack–Tartar War (1667–1671), War of Devolution (France, Spain, Dutch, England, Swedish) (1667–1668), Stepan Razin Rebellion (1667), Angelets (France vs Tax Resisters) (1667–1675), Solovetsky Monastery uprising (1668–1676), Shakushain's Revolt (1669–1672), Polish–Ottoman War

(1672–1676), Franco–Dutch War (1672–1678), Third Anglo–Dutch War (1672–1674), Revolt of the Three Feudatories (Qing Empire vs Tungning)(l673–1681), Trunajaya Rebellion (1674–1681), Revolt of the papier timbre (1675), Scanian War (1675–1679), King Philip's War (1675–1678), Revolutions of Tunis (1675–1705), Russo–Turkish War (1676–1681), Dzungar conquest of Altishahr (1678–1680), Tibet–Ladakh–Mughal War (1679–1684), Pueblo Revolt (1680), Maratha–Mughal War (1681–1707), Great Turkish War (1683–1699), Polish–Ottoman War (1683–1699), War of the Reunions (1683–1684), Morean War (1684–1699), Monmouth Rebellion (1685), Second Tarnovo Uprising (1685–1686), Child's War (1686–1690), Russo–Turkish War (1686–1700), Siamese–English War (1687), Revolt of the Barretinas (1687–1689), Crimean campaigns (1687–1689), Dzungar–Qing War (1687–1758), Chiprovtsi Uprising (1688), Nine Years' War (1688–1697), Karposh's Rebellion (1689), King William's War (1689–1697), Willamite War in Ireland (1689–1691), Scottish Jacobite Rising (1689–1692), Second Brotherhood (1693), Komenda Wars (1694–1700), Azov campaigns (1695–1696), Streltsy Uprising (1698), Darien Scheme (1699–1700), Great Northern War (1700–1721), Battle of Dartsedo (1701), War of the Spanish Succession (1701–1714), Queen Anne's War (1702–1713), Camisard Rebellion (1702–1715), Rakoczi's War of Independence (1703–1711), Civil War in Poland (1704–1706), First Javanese War of Succession (1704–1708), Bavarian People's Uprising (1705–1706), Mughal war of succession (1707), Bulavin Rebellion (1707–1708), War of the Emboabas (1707–1709), Hotaki Safavid War (1709–1722), Pruth River Campaign (1710–1711), Battle of Ain Dara (1711), Tuscarora War (1711–1715), Huilliche Rebellion (1712), New York Slave Revolt (1712), Toggenburg War (1712), First Fox War (1712–1716, Ottoman–Venetian War (1714–1718), Yamasee War (South Carolina militia/Cherokee Indians) (1715–1717), Jacobite rising (1715–1716), Omani invasion of Bahrain (1717), War of the Quadruple Alliance (1718–1720), Chinese expedition to Tibet (1720), Attingal Outbreak (India) (1721), Chickasaw Wars (Choctaw, France, British, and Chickasaw Indians) 1712–1763), Father Rale's War (1722–

1725), Russo–Persian War (1722–1723), Ottoman–Persian War (1722–1727), Saltpeter Wars (1726–1745), Appeal War (1726–1727), Anglo–Spanish War (1727–1729), Second Fox War (1728–1733), Patrona Halil Revolt (1730), Ottoman–Persian War (1730–1735), Slave Insurrection on St. John (1733), War of the Polish Succession (1733–1738), Miao Rebellion (Qing dynasty) (1735–1736), Spanish–Portuguese War (1735–1737), Austro–Russian–Turkish War (1735–1739), Bashkir Rebellion (1735–1740), Nadir Shah's invasion of the Mughal Empire (1738–1739), Stono Rebellion (1739), War of Jenkins' Ear (1739–1748), War of the Austrian Succession (1740–1748), First Silesian War (1740–1742), Java War (1741–1743), Russo–Swedish War (1741–1743), Ottoman–Persian War (1743–1746), Chukchi War (1744–1747), King George's War (1744–1748), Second Silesian War (1744–1745), Jacobite rising (1745), First Carnatic WAr (1746–1748), Civil War between Afsharid and Qajar (1747–1796), Second Carnatic War (1749–1754), Konbaung–Hanthawaddy War (1752–1757), French and Indian War (British, Onondaga, Oneida, Seneca, Tuscarora, Mohawk, Cayuga, Catawba, and Cherokee Indians against France, Abenaki, Algonquin, Caughnawaga, Lenape, Mi'kmaq, Ojibwa, Ottawa, Shawnee, and Wyandot Indians (1754–1763), Guarani War (1756), Seven Years' War (1756), Third Silesian War (1756–1763), Third Carnatic War (1757–1763), Pomeranian War (1757–1762), Revolt of the Altishahr Khojas (Qing) (1757–1759), Anglo–Cherokee War (1758–1761), Burmese–Siamese War (1759–1760), Tacky's War (1760), Canek Revolt (1761), Fantastic War (1762–1763), Berbice Slave Uprising (1763–1766), Pontiac's War (1763–1766), Russo–Circassian War (1763–1864), Strilekrigen (1765), Burmese–Siamese War (1765–1767), War of the Regulation (1765–1771), Mysorean Invasion of Kerala (1766–1792), First Anglo–Mysore War (1767–1769), Louisiana Rebellion (1768), Russo–Turkish War (1768–1774), Bar Confederation (1768–1772), First Carib War (1769–1773), Moamoria Rebellion (1769–1806), Moscow plague riot (1771), Sannyasi Rebellion (1772), Pugachev's Rebellion (1773–1775), Lord Dunmore's War (1774), Burmese–Siamese War (1775–1776), First Anglo–Maratha War (1775–1782), American

Revolutionary War (1775–1783), Spanish–Portuguese War (1776–1777), Chickamauga Wars (1776–1794), War of the Bavarian Succession (1778–1779), Anglo–Spanish War (1779–1783), First Xhosa War (1779–1781), Fourth Anglo–Dutch War (1780–1784), Second Anglo–Mysore War (1780–1784), Revolt of the Comuneros (New Granada) (1781), Unrest in Bahrain (1783), Kettle War (1784), Revolt of Horea, Closca, and Crisan (1784), Burmese–Siamese War (1785–1786), Northwest Indian War (1785–1795), Lofthuus' Rebellion (1786–1787), Shays' Rebellion (1786–1787), Prussian invasion of Holland (1787), Burmese–Siamese War (1787), Austro–Turkish War (1787–1791), Russo–Turkish War (1787–1791), Russo–Swedish War (1787–1792), Theater War (1788–1789), Australian frontier wars (European settlers/Indigenous Australians) (1788–1930), Sino–Nepalese War (1788–1792), Battle of Ngoc Hoi-Dong Da (1788–1789), Menashi–Kunashir Rebellion (1789), Third Anglo–Mysore War (1789–1792), Second Xhosa War (1789–1793), Pemulwuy Resistance (1790–1802), Saxon Peasants' Revolt (1790), Haitian Revolution (1791–1804), Whiskey Rebellion (1791–1794), Polish–Russian War (1792), Burmese–Siamese War (1792), War of the First Coalition (1792–1797), War in the Vendee (1793–1796), Tripolitanian Civil War (1793–1796), Cotiote War (1793–1806), Nickajack Expedition (1794), Pazvantoglu Rebellion (1794), Kosciuszko Uprising (1794), White Lotus Rebellion (1794–1804), Battle of Krtsanisi (1795), Hawkesbury and Nepean Wars (1795–1816), Second Carib War (1795–1797), Miao Rebellion (1795–1806), Persian Expedition (1796), Anglo–Spanish War (1796–1808), Burmese–Siamese War (1797), Peasants' War (France) (1798), War of the Second Coalition (1798–1802), Irish Rebellion (1798), Fourth Anglo–Mysore War (1798–1799), Third Xhosa War, (1799–1803), War of the Knives (1799–1800), and not to be forgotten the Quasi-War between the United States and France. (1798–1800.)

Recorded wars: 220
Earth population: Eight hundred million

So much for the Golden Rule and God's other commandants.

Earth's Christian and religious leaders along with the intellects and government leaders of the day bemoaned the wars and the loss of innocent lives, but no serious attempts were made to come to some kind of world order that would outlaw such behavior. Over the next two hundred years (1800 to 2000), the Popes, the European powerhouses, along with the League of Nations and the United Nations tried to exercise such control, but their efforts were complete and utter failures.

God and Jesus discussed the human experiment that was being played out, below them, on earth and were perplexed by the Byzantine mentality that dominated so many of earth's leaders and their policies. God shook his head in disbelief and ask more than once, "How can they (the world's leaders) be so blind and callous to the plight of the average man? Where did we go wrong? What in their make-up makes them so inscrutable and evil? It almost seems that war, and the killing of thousands, is their only solution. Is it Lucifer's work or a major design flaw?"

Jesus, looking perplexed, had no immediate answer to his father's questions; however, later, he shared, "I have noticed that the inhabitants of Teren have a completely different outlook on life, and I think it stems from the fact that they know, with no doubt whatsoever, that you exist and are there to guide their lives. It is proven daily by the fact that your son provides daily and hands-on inspiration. There are no evil thoughts, because they respect your ultimate power and the benevolent existence you have given them. After all, fear of the unknown is a natural human reaction, and on Teren and the recent colonized planets, there is no unknown, thus no fear. No fear means no need for defense, no need for conquest, and no need for any of the negative feelings, because everything is centered around the humane* treatment of self and others."

---

* humane—kind, compassionate, accommodating, altruistic, amiable, approachable, benevolent, benign, benignant, broad-minded, charitable, clement, considerate, cordial, democratic, forbearing, forgiving, friendly, generous, genial, gentle, good, good-natured, gracious, helpful, human humanitarian, indul-

God looked long and hard at his son and liked what he saw. No further words were necessary.

The qualities that all Terenians embraced; the qualities that far too few earthlings practice.

---

gent, kindhearted, kind, lenient, liberal, magnanimous, merciful, mild, natural, obliging, open minded, philanthropic. pitying, righteous, sympathetic, tender, tenderhearted, tolerant, understanding, unselfish, warmhearted (from my Roget's Twenty-First Century Thesaurus).

18

Teren Plus Five Other Planets: 1600 to 2000

The ingenious and creative minds of the humans who inhabited Teren and the other far-flung colonized planets of Alpha, Beta, Gamma, Delta, and Epsilon had in recent years turned their attention to Artificial Intelligence (AIs) machines, and these cybernetic critters came in every size, shape, and description. They quickly wormed their way deep into each venue, becoming an integrated and indispensable part of each unique civilization. The burdens of manual labor, housekeeping, and even cooking were relegated to these AI machines, and the slang expression for this overall body of mechanical creations was "DuErs".

DuErs did everything, and the populations on Teren and the other five planets accepted the fact that humankind no longer had to concern themselves with ditch digging, farming, or any other manual labor task. DuErs were becoming so commonplace that some joked that "sweat might become a thing of the past."

With most manual and repetitive labor relegated to the DuErs, the humans on each planet concerned themselves with management and designing new applications for almost every human endeavor.

Religion, entertainment, sports, travel, and highly developed inventive activities were reserved for the thinking humans. All logical and creative thought sequences evolved from the minds of the humans during the course of their normal daily activities, and the DuErs dutifully carried out its designated and designed assignments.

There were centers scattered throughout every community where people went to study, socialize, and exchange information on related lines of endeavors and to engage in all manner of religious and social activities, including games—not only the physical Olympic types but also mental championships from poker and chess to Wild West Mania, a card and marble game that combined Chinese checkers with cribbage, which were wildly popular. The local champions moved into regional and national championships, and there were even planet against planet levels of competition.

Many people dedicated their lives to working on making DuErs for every human function that the mind could imagine. Since many of these cybernetic machines were designed and built by the so called "little people," many of the robots (AIs) were extremely small and compact. When the "little people" returned to their original size, the miniature factor was even more dramatic.

By the late 1800s, the DuErs were firmly entrenched in every single phase of human activity, and by the end of the century, they were so sophisticated that a DuEr could actually build another DuEr and have unique conversations with their human designers. The indoor DuErs relied on their batteries to breathe life into their movements and activities; however, there were a whole class of outdoor DuErs that required no batteries. A special paint had been developed which doubled as a solar panel, and its only drawback was that it only came in one color: burnt orange. Teams of scientists had tried for years to expand the color range but only the burnt-orange color seemed to be capable, with the other paint components, of turning sunlight into energy, so naturally all the outside DuErs were painted the Golden Gate bridge color as were the outside of every building and structure. From space, each planet grew to have an orange hew as every outdoor structure, machine, conveyance, bridge, and boat doubled as an electrical generating station.

In the year 1898, Jesus of Teren, who enjoyed visiting the other planets, was beginning to notice a change, subtle at first but which seemed to be grew more pronounced with each passing year. The proliferation of DuErs meant that the human component took care of the management activities of leading, planning, organizing, controlling, manufacturing, and related work to bring a product to market, build a building or bridge, or farm a track of land which previously had been relegated to younger unskilled workers. As the cultures developed, these simple jobs where being replaced by DuErs. This did not seem to upset people in that it gave a whole new class of humans the opportunity to become educated, to use their imagine, and to follow their dreams.

Birth now came complete with a promise of education to whatever level one wished to attain and the opportunity to work and maintain a very comfortable standard of living so that everyone could pursue his or her areas of interest. Some people ran businesses, and some were in education and medicine, and it worked out that whatever your particular interest might be, there was a way for you to peruse your goals without worrying about food and shelter and clothing. To qualify for a house, food rations or apparel or whatever one needed, each person had a credit-card chip placed underneath the skin on the back of their right hand, and this card, inserted at birth, had almost unlimited purchasing power and a bill was never forthcoming. The system was not abused, because greed was no longer a part of the human experience. The Ten Commandments were the basis for all interactivity, and no one violated the tenants. At the end of your life, i.e., upon death, your skin card was removed, and the assets you controlled were returned to the providers. There were of course provisions for spouses and families, but over the long haul, the provider of goods received those goods back, be it a house or a people-moving vehicle, an airplane, or a diamond ring.

It was not a foolproof system, but it had evolved through trial and error, over the centuries and was now an accepted way of life. There were still rich people, who owned physical assets and land but there were no poor people, no homeless and no cries of injustice from any quarter of the population. Regardless of your specific areas of interest, everyone was encouraged to find a focus in life and to pursue that focus or dream, letting it take the dreamers to wherever it might lead. It was an exciting time, and most people seemed to think that a utopian level had finally been reached by the human race under Jesus's direct and hands-on guidance.

The DuErs, i.e., the highly sophisticated and almost thinking ones, watch the human activities and actually thought about their place in the society. More and more, they were responsible for building and maintaining and keeping the wheels of commerce turning, yet they had no say in anything and were, as far as humankind was concerned, just another machine.

Decades passed into centuries, and the technical advancements, by man and his machines, was truly beyond comprehension. By 2000, DuErs were actually designing associates and having intelligent give-and-take conversations and communications with their human masters. Imagine, if you will, the construction of a new class of space vehicles where the human input sets up a chain of specifications that teams of engineers developed over years of trial and error only to be baulked at by the chief construction and design DuEr.

"Humans," addressed to a meeting of space engineers and high-ranking space management types at the space launch center near Baghdad in a matter of fact mechanical voice, the DuEr explained, "My databank, drawn from six million data storage facilities around the world, indicates that you should scrap the nuclear power plants that have dominated space travel since shortly after man first escaped the bonds of Teren's gravity and flung himself into space. My fellow AIs think you should consider a new rocket engine that draws upon electric power and magnetic fields to channel superheated plasma out the exhaust. This stream of plasma generates steady, efficient thrust that uses low amounts of propellant and builds up speed over time This, according to all the data bases will let us not only increase our payloads but the transit time to reach Teren-Alpha will only be forty days whereas the trip now requires to seven months. I have cross checked this with all design and engineering DuErs and our recommendation is unanimous."

Shocked humans stared at the speaking DuEr; human eye met human eye and perplexed expressions flashed around the conference table. This was not the first time a DuEr had suggested an alternate approach, but this was a quantum leap that the humans had not contemplated. The team leader asked, "Are you certain the data that lead you to this recommendation is accurate?"

"Absolutely," and then added in the monotone voice, "Scientists in America and Asia have been experimenting with this electric propulsion system, and their ion engines create thrust based on energized gas. The VASIMR system (variable-specific impulse magneto plasma rocket) uses ionized gases such as xenon or hydrogen to create superheated plasma stream for thrust." Continuing the DuEr added, "The VASIMR system also has the advantage of relying upon electromagnetic waves to create and energize the plasma, rather than physical electrodes that get worn down due to their contact with the superheated plasma. That, of course translates into greater reliability over time and allows for a very dense plasma stream to create even more thrust. Not hesitating to nail home the point the DuEr finished by explaining that, "The VASIMR system can also adjust its thrust to speed up or slow down, and even has an 'afterburner' mode that provides a temporary high-speed boost at the cost of efficiency, of course."

Looking at his colleges the human leader had to admit, "I think we all agree that the pre-atomic chemical rockets that burn solid or liquid chemical propellants won't get us deep into space because they just require too much propellant and the atomic units have their drawbacks with regard to the radioactive waste their spent fuel rods represent, but I am wondering if this is a necessary change at this point in time?"

Opinions from the team members ranged from outright rejection of the DuEr's recommendations to fully embracing the concept, and the meeting was adjourned with an agreement that the team members would return to their home bases and come up with recommendations and that they would meet in six months to continue their discussions. In the meantime, the DuEr was directed to create an electronic paper that would set forth, in detail, the concepts of the VASIMR system and disseminate it to all interested agencies, worldwide.

Jesus had just returned from a trip to all the planets and was sharing his experiences with God, who smiled at the revelations being described in that he already knew the details. (God, of course, could monitor every happening on every planet without missing a single word.) He, however, let Jesus described the DuEr situation in detail and at a convenient break asked, "Where do you see humans going with this AI explosion?"

"I think it's just a matter of time until they create AI's that can actually think, that is replicating the human brain function into the seventy-five to eighty percentile range.

"Will there ever be a point where the AI's will want to become the dominate partner?"

Jesus looked at his father, the creator of everything in the endless universe, and pondered the question for some time before answering.

"Father, I think the humans are smart enough to preclude designing human emotions into their AI's but that does not mean that a super intelligent AI could not design that function into his fellow AI's."

The father looked at his son and replied, "Our humans on earth are centuries behind but they are starting to replicate what is going on Teren and the other inhabited planets. I don't worry about the Terenans and their colonies, because we have created a society where evil is unknown, but I am concerned that the evil at work on earth could bring their brand of devilment to the AI's. and that could be very devastating for the earth's human population, Of course that will be many years in the future but it is something to ponder and watch."

"What will you do?"

"Well son, at this point, we will have to just let it play out, but these certainly are developments that may move up our schedule for your brother returning to earth."

19

Earth: 1800 to 2018

On the blue planet named Earth, tripping around our small sun, just one of the billions God placed in the universe, the human population grew from one billion in 1800 to 6.1 billion a fifth of the way into the twenty-first century.

Of the current totals about thirty-one percent of the world's population are Christian, twenty-four percent follow the Islam faith, fifteen percent are Hindus, and the remaining thirty percent are divided between hundreds of sects and nonbelievers. Sometime this century, Islam will replace Christianity as the dominant religion on the planet, and God and Jesus of Nazarene have long engaged in perplexing discussions about the human experience and how the drama may or may not play out. The lively exchanges include scenarios of the time frame for Jesus returning to earth in his human form.

The experiment on Teren has proven beyond a shadow of a doubt that humankind's inhumanity toward his fellow traveler, which is so evident on earth, does not have to be part of the human life experience.

The Teren populations and those that have spread to the five other planets experience none of the greed, killing and demagoguery that seems to run unchecked on earth as Satan has been thwarted on Teren and the other five planets, by the ever present and hands-on leadership of Jesus of Nazarenes twin brother.

During the nineteenth and twentieth centuries earths dominate life form charged ahead through the industrial revolution and into the information age, but not without a great deal of pain, suffering and death. In just two hundred years humans engaged in 515 wars and thousands upon thousands of lesser conflicts that left millions dead, remembered only by those that remained to endure the consequences of their slaughter.

(In the prologue, the earth wars from 1800 to present were listed and as you read this book, there are people, this very second, being killed, all over the planet, in the name of some religion or to further the claim of some sanguinary leader or to enrich a perpetrator. Does life have to contain these elements? All the great and wise minds on earth seem to think so or they would have taken definitive action within the two thousand years since Jesus died for our sins. Fearless, God fearing men of earth would have risen up and demanded an end to slavery. in its many forms, to death and destruction from war and to crime, in all its forms. We humans hear about it daily but it's all talk. The United Nations stands by and with wringing hands condemns the actions but there are never consequences, only more ambagious talk.)

Deep within earth's moon entered from a camouflaged impact crater, the Russians named Patsaev (coordinates 16.7 S 133.4 E), on the dark side of the earth's constant troll, a group of scientists from the planet Teren have been studying the earth and its peoples for the past six hundred years. The Russian satellite Luna took the first pictures of the far side of the moon in 1959, and the Terenian scientists were amused that the earthlings had no clue that the crater they named Patsaev, after cosmonaut Viktor Patsayev who died in the Soyuz 11 mission, served as the entrance to their secret observation base. The Terenians have even gone so far as to send spies to live among the earthlings, but that is the subject of a future book. (or so I am told).

When the earth was first discovered, everyone on Teren and the five other planets were excited beyond any level one could imagine. The news organizations, universities' thinkers and scholars, and indeed the entire population were eager to establish contact with the new planet that was almost identical to mother Teren. Jesus, of course, knew what they had discovered but kept the information to himself, interested to see how his people would handle this new mind-altering discovery. The continents, the oceans, the rivers, and the flora and fauna were all carbon copies of Teren as were the humans, but there was a difference that was very evident, even from space, which gave the Terenians real cause for concern.

When the Terenians' spaceships first discovered earth and entered its atmosphere, on high-speed reconnaissance runs, it was painfully obvious that the primary life form, which inhabited this beautiful agate, were extremely proficient war makers. On one of the major continents, they discovered a battle raging and by day's end, seven thousand of the combatants lay dead or dying on a blood-drenched muddy field, surrounded by the exquisite beauty of the fall colors, the brilliant blue sky, and the autumn clouds that floated by.

The Terenians could not believe their eyes and chose not to let their presence be known. Why would you want to subject Terenians to such stone age brutality? It may have been the same impression Captain Cook got when he first found the beautiful and idyllic Hawaiian Islands and encountered the fierce warriors of Hawaii who might show an English sailor how to fish and the next minute could bash his brains out with a club, cook him and eat him.

The initial flybys and incursions established without question that much of earth's population were engaged in some form of geno-cidal activity, and this immediately sent up warning signs that would make exploration a very slow and tedious undertaking. The moon base was established so that the Terenians could study the earthlings, before making any direct contact.

By the middle of the 1900, hundreds of the Terenians concluded that earth and its humans were something to avoid, like the plague. Much of the world was engaged in a world war that impacted every single person residing on the planet. Watching the inhumanity going on in Germany, Asia, and the Pacific on such a grand scale and the wholesale death and destruction being wrecked on the planets human populations, it was a no brainier for the Terenians to pass on revealing their presence to the earthlings. The carnage they watched was unparalleled in human history. Over twenty-seven thousand people died each day between the start of World War II and the end of the conflict. In just five years and one day the war to end wars accounted for the deaths of over 60 million people. (Since 1945 over nine million Americans have been killed in wars, all over the blue planet.)

Back on Mother Teren, the leaders and Jesus discussed the situation in detail, and there were late-night debates as to what the best course of action might entail. Some urged Jesus to reappear on earth and put an end to the killing and the religious strife, but others maintained that it was too late, and they should write off earth, close their moon base, and concentrate on other areas in the nearby solar system.

One thoughtful older scholar looked directly at Jesus and ask," On earth, they have what they call the Christian religion and they study a book called the Bible which is a collection of stories about the life and death of a person they called Jesus of Nazarene as well as about how humans should treat and interact with one another. Their Ten Commandments are almost identical to our Ten Commandments and I wonder if you can explain how such two far flung civilizations could be so similar, in some ways and so different in others?"

Jesus smiled and looking into the heavens for guidance began slowly in a soft unassuming voice. Every person in the room was on the edge of their seats and a pin dropping would have seemed like a clap of thunder. "Thank you for such a thoughtful question." Looking around the room he continued, "My father, God Almighty, creator of heaven and Teren and all the stars and constellations, in fact the entire universe wondered when you first ventured into space if one day you would discover the existence of earth."

Looking at the thoughtful intelligent faces, hanging on his every word Jesus continued, "When God created the universe he decided to create two planets, where his image's might grow and develop and for thousands of years life on earth and life on Teren took almost identical paths, however when I and my twin brother were born our father decided to send us to the parallel planets as the human race, on both planets, needed help and guidance to find a way out of their pagan and satanical practices. They were lost in the history of the past and Rome and its zest to conquer the world was consuming most of the planets treasure and this, of course, had a devastating effects on the human population. Previously God had sent many messengers but they were all mortal men and while they did their best they could not overcome the heresy and evil practices going on in the parallel worlds."

Pausing to let his previous words sink in Jesus continued, "In order to show the peoples of each world the path that God would like them to follow he sent myself and my twin brother to each of the parallel planets and we preached to the people, not the leaders, but to the people and ask them to follow us. In both worlds the threatened leaders could not allow us to continue and God having foreseen this outcome allowed my brother and myself to be crucified."

The Terenian leaders listening where amazed at these firsthand revelations and could not wait for Jesus to continue.

"God plan was that if he allowed us (his sons) to die and then raised us from the dead, to sit on either side of him throughout eternity that then redemption would be available to all men, for their sins and transgressions. The Christian faithful, with the Bible as the revered handbook has been engaged in spreading the word of redemption and salvation to all the peoples of the planet, for the last two thousand years, yet at this point in time Christians make up only about a third of the earth's population. In fact by the end of the twenty-first century there will be more Islam followers than Christians and if Islam follows past practices they will do all in their power to eliminate all non-Islam believers from planet earth as their Quran directs.

"Will God allow that to happen," the older scholar excitably ask and then immediately realized that he may have over stepped and put on a demure grin. Jesus just smiled and softly replied, "No, God my father will not let that happen but I cannot tell you, at this time, how history will record the actions and interactions that will be forthcoming."

After a long and somewhat awkward silence Jesus continued, "Fear not my lambs. God did not set all this in motion, since the beginning of time, to let it all be negated by a religion whose esteemed founder languishes in the deepest darkest depths of hell."

EPILOGUE

Major Muslim Wars

B
attle of Dadar (624) where the Quran states that Allah sent an "unseen army of Angels" that helped the Muslims def eat the Meccans. Expedition of Waddan (623), Patrol of Buwat (623), Expedition of AI Ashirah (623), First Expedition to Badar (623), Battle of Bodor (624, Invasion of Sawiq (624), Invasion of Banu Qaynuqa (624), Al Kudr Invasion (624), Invasion of Bahran (624), Battle of Uhud (625), Invasion of Hamra al-Asad (625), Invasion of Banu Nadir (625), Expedition of Dhat al-Riqa, Invasion of Badr (626), Invasion of Dumatul Jandal (626), Battle of the Trench (627), Invasion of Banu Qurayza (627), Invasion of Banu-Lahuan (627), Treaty of Hudaybiyyah (628), Battle of Khaybar (628), Third Expedition of Wadi al Qura, Conquest of Mecca (629) Battle of Hunayn (630), Battle of Autos (630), Siege of Ta'if (630), Battle of Tabouk (630), Death of Muhammad (632).

Interesting that Jesus spent his life preaching and teaching; caused the death of no one, whereas Muhammad engaged in twenty-five bloody wars in his short lifetime and was and is responsible for the deaths of millions of Christian and non-Islam believers.

Holy war against Persians (634), Conquest against Syria and Persia. Syria falls in (641), Persia in (642), Byzantine forces recapture Alexandria from Arabs (645), Arabs recapture Alexandria (646), Conquer Cyprus (649), Defeat Byzantiane fleet at Battle of the Masts to take control of Mediterranean for first time. (655), Siege of

Constantinople which starts (673) and continues thru (678) without success. War against Christian Coptic Egyptians (640–655), War against Berbers–North Africans (650–700), War against the Spanish (711–730), War against Franks (modern France) (720–723), Sicilians War (812–940), War against Chinese (751), Armenian/Georgians war (1071–1291), Crusade against Jihad (1096–1260), War against Hindus in India, Pakistan and Bangladesh (638–1857), Jihad against Poland (1444–1699), War against Rumania (1350–1699), Jihad against Russia (1500–1853), Jihad against Bulgaria (1350–1843), Jihad against Serbs, Croats and Albanians (1334–1920), Jihad against Greeks (1450–1853), Jihad against Albania (1332–1851), Jihad against Croatia (1389–1843), Jihad against Israelis (1948–present). Between 650 and 1050, in Central Asia, these four hundred years were the fieriest in the Turkish struggle against the Islamic Jihad. Over the years the pagan turks were transformed into Muslims and later became Jihad's themselves to carry the bloodied tradition of aggression and forcible conversion into Anatolis (modern Turkey) and through the Balkans up to Austria and Poland.

While all forms of religious fanaticism are negative, only Islam raises slaughter of all Kafirs (non-Muslims) to a holy creed, as it teaches Muslims to gloat over the killing of non-Muslims and celebrate their death. Hence Islam is the most demented and dangerous form of religious fanaticism. It is not Islamic fanaticism that is to be blamed for this, as Islam itself is fanaticism.

What is Jihad? The Arabic word Jihad is derived from the root word Jahada (struggle). Jihad has come to mean an offensive war to be waged by Muslims against all non-Muslims to convert them to Islam on the pain of death. Jihad is enjoined on all Muslims by the Quran.

In heaven, Jesus and God discuss the turmoil.

Earth Jesus to God: I have been watching and studying and cannot come to any basic rationalization regarding the conflicts between the Christians and the Muslims. Can you help me understand why since, the seventh century, those two parties have not been able to moderate their views or at least come to some kind of an agreement that would stop the bloodshed and the loss of innocent lives, on both side of the issue?

God: Well Son that is a question I too have pondered and I think you have to look deep into the beliefs of each camp to find the answer as well as into the makeup of the human. It has occurred to me that neither side can live in peace as long as the Muslims hold fast to their core ideals. I see Christians trying to extend the olive branch by encouraging the Muslims to live within the Christian societies but it does not seem to work. The Muslims religion is just not flexible. They operate under such a staunch set of rules of conduct which does not let them vary, in the slightest, from the words and laws set down in their Quran. For example, the Quran, 2:256 states that no other religion will be accepted other than Islam, so it is difficult for them to live in countries where Christian laws and morality are practiced by the majority. You certainly do not see many non-Muslims immigrating to Muslim countries because the nonbelievers could not survive under the strict Muslim rules.

Jesus: Assuming that is the case why then do the Muslims choose to live in the Christian and Pagan countries? Why don't they just stay in those lands that they dominate.

God: I can think of only one reason.

Jesus: And what would that be?

God: They are driven by a single goal which is worldwide domination, to the exclusion of all other points of view. Son, there are over one hundred and two verses, in the Quran, that call Muslims to war with nonbelievers for the sake of Islamic rule. Some are graphic, with commands to chop off heads and fingers and to kill infidels wherever they may be found. Those Muslims that do not join the fight are called hypocrites and warned that their God Allah will send them to hell if they do not join in the slaughter.

Jesus: Are there any parts of the Quran that do not call for such violence and demoniac actions?

God: Unfortunately, there are very few verses of tolerance and peace to balance out the many that call for nonbelievers to be fought and subdued until they either accept humiliation, convert to Islam, or are killed.

Picking up a worn copy of a large-format book, God slowly turned the pages and upon finding the passage he was looking for he quoted, "Verses (2:191–193) read as follows: 'And kill them wherever you find them and turn them out from where they have turned you out. And AI Fitnah (their disbelief) is worse than killing, but if they desist, then lo Allah is forgiving and merciful. And fight them until there is no more Fitnah (disbelievers) and worship is for Allah alone.'

Jesus: Is there any common ground politically, philosophically, spiritually or even socially?

God: Politically each Muslim believer must submit to the mullahs and since they teach annihilation of any nonbelievers. I would not think a political solution is possible. Philosophically the answer has to again be no since the Quran does not allow freedom of religion and expression and therefore democracy and Islam cannot coexist. Every Muslim government is either dictatorial or autocratic. Spiritually has to be no as well because I am referred to as loving and kind, no such descriptions of Allah are contained anywhere in the Quran. The last category was socially, and I am afraid that has to be a no as well because Muslims allegiance to Islam forbids them to make friends with Christians, Jews or any class of nonbelievers.

Jesus: So what would you propose to overcome such straight forward dogma?

God: I have been thinking on that since Muhammad came to prominence and there is no easy solution. It is obvious that I could send you down to show them the error of their expansionist ways but then all the deaths since the Muslims first started expanding North, East and West would have been pointless. I always hoped that man might solve these conflicts without my interference.

Looking at his son and noting the serious and concerned look on his face the Father continued: "It was around earth's year eleven hundred, when Europe finally came to the breaking point. The Muslim conquerors had not only killed hundreds of thousands of Christian, over the last five hundred years, but made slaves and eunuchs of them for the pleasure of the caliphs. The Muslim imperialist colonialist conquest burned and sacked the holy churches, robbed, killed and pillaged the people of Jerusalem and the surrounding areas. The

Pope decided to free the people of the Holy Lands from their brutal masters and to reclaim Christianity's holiest places for free Christians to worship. It is true that some of the Crusaders were barbaric and evil but it was a normal human reaction to the total carnage that the Muslims had perpetrated on their fellow Christians. All these centuries I had hoped that the Christian values would be a strong enough magnet to overcome the darkness of Islam but my assessment, of Islam's strength and popularity, may have been incorrect."

Pausing, God looked down at Teren and then continued, "I now believe that your brothers presence is the only thing that keeps the peoples of Teren on the peaceful, non-confrontational track. Should I recall him tomorrow I think it would only be a matter of time until competing groups would find areas of disagreement and the planet would evolve back into an earth-like model."

Pausing and with a long sad face that made Jesus want to cry, God conjectured, "It just may be that when I created humankind I gave them too much of a competitive spirit. Just too competitive for their own good and that striving, clawing natural piece of their makeup, which may be almost as powerful as the propagation drive, has led them to the outcome we see being played out on earth today."

Jesus: What will you do, Father?"

God: I am not certain. The Christians of earth have been waiting for your return, as I set forth, and promised in the scriptures, and I just may fulfill that prophecy. After all son it was you who said, 'Let not your heart be troubled; you believe in God, believe also in Me. In My Father's house are many mansions: if it were not so, I would have told you. I go to prepare a place for you. And if I go and prepare a place for you, I will come again and receive you to Myself; that where I am, there you may be also.' John 14:1–3 I think," he said with a smile.

Pausing, which saw a decade pass on earth, God put his arm around his son's shoulder, looked deep into his crystal blue eyes and said with an upbeat voice, "Now let's go find your Mother and see what she has to say on this subject."

ABOUT THE AUTHOR

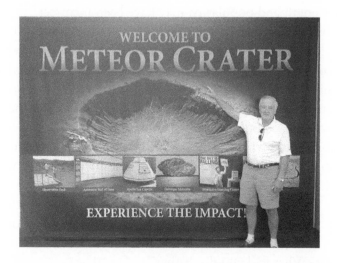

J ack D. Waggoner spent a lifetime traveling Asia and America selling and installing American tire-and-rubber-manufacturing equipment from his base in Kailua, Hawaii, and Sacramento, California. During his military service, he served aboard the aircraft carrier USS *Philippine Sea* (CVA-47) and was in Hiroshima, just nine years after the atomic bomb was dropped on the city. The devastation of Tokyo and Hiroshima made a lasting impression on the young American sailor and were subthemes in two of his published books, *Bird Nest* and *The Rainbow Zhanlue (Strategy)*. Other yet to be published works are *Fight to Puska, Killing ISIS,* and *The Voyages Under Arcturus.*

During his time in Hawaii, Jack became an avid ocean fisherman and manufactured a line of marlin lures. These days, you can find him exploring the back reaches of Lake Mead, Lake Mohave, and the Colorado River from his home in Laughlin, Nevada.